the Journey of the Magi

Maryann Costa Beckman

ISBN-10: 0979088666
ISBN-13: 978-0979088667

DEDICATION

This book is dedicated to all the wise men I know, most notably my father; to Josh for his constant faith in me, to Len for his support and encouragement; and to all those who are daring enough to go on the journey.

Contents

THE TRADITION

Balaam, the infamous prophet from Mesopotamia, was an early member of the magi. It is rumored by some that he was even the founder. It was Balaam's prophecy, as recorded in the Torah, which spoke of a future star that would herald a change unlike any the world had ever known. Here is his prophecy, actually forced by God to be uttered against the prophet's own will:

> "I shall see Him, but not now: I shall behold Him, but not nigh: there shall come a Star out of Jacob, and a Sceptre shall rise out of Israel, and shall smite the corners of Moab, and destroy all the children of Sheth, and Edom shall be a possession. Seir also shall be a possession for his enemies; and Israel shall do valiantly. Out of Jacob shall come He that shall have dominion, and shall destroy him that remaineth of the city."

> (Numbers 24:17-19)

The magi remembered these words. They grew in renown and craft. Men from other lands traveled great distances to seek their council. Some called them priests while others called them seers and magicians. They were all these things, and more. It was the magi that reached into the darkness and touched the spirits. It was the magi that dared to look where other men would not see. It was the magi that could take an ordinary man and proclaim him king.

Then, they were challenged by Nebuchadnezzar. This old king dreamed a disturbing dream. It plagued him, but he would not share its contents. No, he demanded the wise ones to reveal to him the contents of his dream, and then interpret its meaning.

Using all their resources, the magi tried. They looked to the stars and used the magic of their potion, but they could find no answers, even under the threat of annihilation.

Then Daniel, a captive and servant in the king's court, intervened.

Daniel said that his God had showed him Nebuchadnezzar's dream and allowed him to understand its meaning. When he was taken before the king, his words were divinely inspired. They sprang to his lips, allowing him to describe the dream and give the interpretation.

Nebuchadnezzar was pleased. The magi were spared and Daniel was appointed Rab Mag, an honored position. There was no higher amongst the magi.

Daniel, an Israelite, never lost sight of his God, even though he would never return to the home of his ancestors. Then Daniel had his own prophetic dream. Before his death, Daniel called his most trusted Magi to his side. When these few had gathered, he gave them the command to protect and pass down the prophecy until it came to pass.

"Remember these words," Daniel instructed. Then he revealed the prophecy:

> "Seventy weeks are determined upon thy people and upon thy holy city, to finish the transgression, and to make an end of sins, and to make reconciliation for iniquity, and to bring in everlasting righteousness, and to seal up the vision and prophecy, and to anoint the most Holy.

> Know therefore and understand, that from the going forth of the commandment to restore and to build Jerusalem unto the Messiah the Prince shall be seven weeks, and threescore and two weeks: the street shall be built again, and the wall, even in troublous times.

> And after threescore and two weeks shall Messiah be cut off, but not for himself: and the people of the prince that shall come shall destroy the city and the sanctuary; and the end thereof shall be with a flood, and unto the end of the war desolations are determined.

> And he shall confirm the covenant with many for one week: and in the midst of the week he shall cause the sacrifice and the oblation to cease, and for the overspreading of abominations he shall make it desolate, even until the consummation, and that determined shall be poured upon the desolate"

> (Daniel 9:24-27)

For over four hundred years, the prophecy was passed down as the Rab Mag had instructed.

This is the story of the magi.

BALTHAZAR

He stood beneath the window watching the sky, a tall, dark man of about forty years. He had inquisitive eyes set near together under a heavy brow. Known as Balthazar; he was known as one who spoke little and laughed even less. Respected by all because of his reputation, he was the highest authority on the movement of the stars.

His place was in the highest room in the highest tower of the temple. In the quiet of this room he would pass his days, seated by the window that faced west. It was in the late hours of the night when he would do most of his work. Because of this, he had few friends and family.

Left alone with only his thoughts, he was able to add to the knowledge of the kingdom. Young magi studying astrology would seek his advice, but they would be turned away. No, he preferred the stars to people.

Balthazar sensed someone standing nearby as he polished his instruments, preparing them for his nightly watch. Ever so slowly he glanced up. It was just as he had predicted. Bardan, the young magus, was attempting his soothsaying skills once

again. He was the most persistent of the lot, visiting Balthazar daily in the high tower. Bardan had even started to practice in his tower room which absolutely irritated Balthazar.

Bardan had been attempting a potion and by the look of
things, had been unsuccessful. *How many times had he tried
this potion? What was the young magus attempting to prove?*
This time, he wiped some sort of liquid on his long robes as
he complained.

"It didn't work," Bardan explained.

"Try another potion then," Balthazar impatiently suggested as he adjusted a piece of glass inside one of his instruments. Balthazar had no interest in conjuring or potions. It
was too imprecise and unpredictable.

*What can you get from throwing ingredients into a bowl
and uttering some unintelligible phrases?*

Bardan did not say anything as he moved back to his
work. He set aside the potions and moved to a group of
bones. Dropping them again and again he studied them, attempting to foretell the future.

Bones, what could dried bones possibly tell him?

Balthazar's own father had been much more interested in
potions and probably would have been able to help Bardan if
he was still alive. *They would have gotten along very well,* he
thought to himself as he looked at Bardan.

"Come, let us practice together" his father would always
say. Not a fan of the occult practices, Balthazar preferred to
study what he could see. As a child he had learned to read
written text and now knew five languages, including Greek.
He read book after book, grasping every bit of tangible
knowledge his mind could hold.

*If only the young magus had the patience for sky-watch-
ing.* It took a great deal of patience to watch the sky night
after night.

The other magus, Bardan, was in his early twenties,
half his age with a face that had just passed boyhood. He
believed in everything, but not for too long. Ambitious and

eager, he was still trying to find his place among the magi.

Balthazar would have spoken to Bardan's father about the interruptions, but the young magus had been orphaned at an early age. This is why Balthazar protested less at his presence than the others.

Carefully, he put aside his instrument and unraveled his star charts. After he slowly unraveled his precious scrolls, he bent over again to continue his work. Steady hands plotted the events of the last few days. It was unusual. He was bothered by what he had seen in the sky.

What does this mean? Could it mean anything at all?

Balthazar searched through the histories to find similar occurrences. He had witnessed unusual star formations over the last nine months. It started with the movements of the King Planet and the King Star. Seventeen days ago the King Planet rose in the rays of dawn in Cancer. It had continued to be seen then five nights ago as Jupiter and Venus rose at dawn as one ball of light in Leo. It was brilliant to behold. The sky was brightened. No doubt other sky watchers had seen the same thing. He had never seen anything like it before, but he was driven to understand. This puzzle had to be solved.

The thought drove him forward. Hiding his face from Bardan, Balthazar continued to study. His eyes grew heavy from the work and his back ached from sitting up night after night. The last few days had been filled with constant work and little rest. It was apparent fatigue was overtaking him. He even considered taking his findings to the others.

What is happening?

Stars followed patterns. Some patterns took months even years, but they *were* predictable. What he had seen in the sky these last few months followed no pattern he knew. He had considered telling his young friend Caspar. He wondered what Caspar would say. The young magus would undoubtedly tell his father, who would tell the other fire-worshippers… No, he had to find the answer first. The others would inevitably find some supernatural meaning. They would attribute it to one god or another. Then they would have a ritual ceremony…or someone would have a dream.

His excitement caused him to push through his fatigue and continue to work. Balthazar was facing a *challenge*. There was a way to explain the occurrences, and he would find an explanation.

Pausing, he looked up. Bardan was nowhere to be seen. *Good.*

CASPAR

Caspar walked into his uncle Varaz's home. This time he entered the stone dwelling more quickly than usual. Most times he would stop and smell the fragrant roses that his aunt Layah had lovingly cultivated and, of course, have something to eat. His aunt and mother would have some food ready for him. His mother preferred to cook in the company of her sisters. It was much more formal at his house and she refused to cook with the servants. The two sisters would laugh and tell stories in Layah's kitchen. He never knew what they discussed, but could hear the laughter echoing through the house. Caspar's interests lay more in line with those of his father: politics and religion. Undoubtedly, this meeting would be about one of those subjects, or both.

As Caspar walked into the house he instantly felt at home. The walls were painted a bright blue and the floor was covered with blue tiles painted with yellow hand-painted designs. Colorful art from Egypt and Greece hung on the walls. It was a house that radiated joy.

"Hello, my nephew," Varaz greeted him heartily as he

entered the house, "welcome."

Caspar walked down the hall toward the large ceremony room. As he walked toward the room, he could hear Varaz greet the others in his usual way.

"Welcome my friend," he said peacefully.

Varaz would give the same greeting nine more times as each man entered the house.

There were many different beliefs among the magi. Some trusted only the signs they were given, others worshipped the Persian gods, others the gods of the Babylonians, the fire-worshippers who followed Zoroaster, and he even heard that there were a few that worshipped the God of Israel, though he did not know any personally.

The last person to enter was Varaz's brother and Caspar's father, Mithradata. Caspar knew all of these men very well because their families were nobles. All were dressed finely; it was the "duty of their station" his father would say to "present themselves well". Each wore a chain with a winged circle of gold. The medallions bore the sign of the followers of Zoroaster.

Caspar was dressed just as the others: in a long silk tunic covered by a robe. A pointed cap rested on his head, allowing his brown hair to flow from underneath. The beard could not hide the youth from his eyes. "The young priest", that is what they had called him.

The men took their places in front of a small flame that was burning in a carved altar in the room. They took turns, as they always had, feeding the flame with wood and fragrant oils. They fanned the flame and as they did, it grew larger.

As the fire grew, they began the ancient chant the Yasura. They began quietly, slowly, then their voices grew. The fire grew as well, taller and stronger until the whole room was filled with light and sound. Caspar watched the flames as they began to dance. There was something hypnotic about the movement of the flames. Growing higher, it moved as if dancing to an unheard song. Caspar watched as the patterns of the flame lulled him into a peaceful state. He could feel the heat of the fire on his face, the sound of the chant against his ear. The sound outside him joined the sound inside and for those few moments, it felt as if everything in the room was one.

In time the song ended and all were seated on the divan in the room. Argian, the elder amongst them, stood and began to speak.

"We are now focused. May the Light that we have looked upon reflect in our own lives." He paused looking at each of the men in the room. "I have called you all together because I believe this is a time of great wonders. The God of Purity who we worship as fire sends us signs in many ways. That is why we look to the ancient elements to tell us what is to come. We yield to the wind, the water, and of course to the fire. I have been studying the signs in the stars."

There was a murmur of interest among the listeners. Caspar was interested. *The stars?* He thought only the astrologers studied the stars.

"The stars," said Argian, "send us messages from the Eternal. They bring light. There is a darkness growing in the world. We are plagued with men who would rely on their own knowledge and think themselves to be gods, including our king. Our scriptures tell us that this will come to pass, and that men will see the brightness of a great light!"

Stars? Caspar's thoughts drifted to Balthazar. *Could he know something?*

Argian continued, "We know the prophecy of the men of the first magi---of Balaam the son of Beor was one of the mightiest. Hear the words of his prophecy: 'There shall come a star out of Jacob, and a scepter shall arise out of Israel.' "

"I do not like this," Godarz, another well-respected Zoroastrian priest interjected, "We should not continue to look for someone outside of the magi. The political climate is changing. We should focus on increasing our influence in the magistrate and in Parthia!"

Some of the others nodded their head in agreement. It was clear that some thought the same as Godraz, but there were a few that agreed with Argian.

"That is true." the voice of Caspar's father, Mithradata filled the room. "We all know the prophecy of the Avesta. It says, 'He shall be the victorious benefactor by name and world-renovator by name. He will benefit the entire physical world; he will establish the physical living existence indestructible. He will oppose the evil of the progeny of the biped and withstand the enmity produced by the faithful. A mighty brightness will surround him, and he shall make life everlasting, incorruptible, immortal for the dead shall rise again.'"

The men clearly respected Mithradata. He was a noble, a priest, and considered to be a wise man. Even as a child Caspar could remember the older men coming to ask his father questions. Not only was he wise in the ways of the faith, he was a great politician. He had been called to council Phraates and his father before him.

"Judah was held captive by the waters of Babylon, and the sons of Jacob were in bondage to our kings. The tribes of Israel are scattered through the mountains like lost sheep, and from the remnant that dwells in Judea under the yoke of Rome neither star nor scepter shall arise."

"And yet," Mithradata interjected, "it was the Hebrew Daniel who was named the mighty interpreter of dreams, the counselor of kings. He was honored by the wise Nebuchadnezzar and our great and beloved King Cyrus. His power was undeniable."

Godarz protested, "He was not a magus! He was a *Hebrew*."

"A Hebrew who knew more than our magi," Mithradata countered, "and who saved the lives of our forefathers. Do not forget that the king was about to kill us all before Daniel intervened. If it were not for him, we would not be here."

There was a murmur that went through the group. Some obviously agreed and held Daniel in high regard.

Mithradata continued, "This is not the place for gossip or irrelevant conversations. If what he says is true then it is true. Daniel proved himself to our people, he does not need to do it again. Remember the words that he wrote: 'Know, therefore, and understand that from the going forth of the command-ment to restore Jerusalem, unto the Anointed One, the Prince, the time shall be seven and threescore and two weeks.' "

"But even the prophecy is vague! I have heard it with my own ears though the followers think it is a secret. The numbers could be interpreted to mean anything," Godarz protested.

"Perhaps, but I have been speaking to the priest Mel-chior." This caused an immediate uproar amongst the men:

"Melchior! He is not a Zoroastrian."

"No, but he is a respected magus!"

"I've heard that he worships the Hebrew God!" Godarz countered.

The group was aghast at the thought: *The Hebrew God!* There were those had dared to compare their religion to that of the Hebrews. Their religion was older and some of the priests even claimed that the Hebrews took their ideas and claimed them for their own. The idea that a magi would wor-ship as the Hebrews was abhorrent to them.

Mithradata continued, "He spoke first to Argian, then to me. Melchior told me that this prophecy is revealing itself, *now.*" He looked at Godarz. "The timing of the prophecy coincides with these strange occurrences in the sky. If you have been studying the stars, you know of these unusual hap-penings."

Again Caspar's thoughts went to Balthazar. Bardan had told him that the magus had been working through the night for many months. *What had he seen?*

Argian spoke, "We have studied the sky, and in the spring of the year we saw conjunction among three planets, occur-ring in the constellation of Pisces the Fish which represents the house of the *Hebrews*. Melchior says that this is a great sign. I believe him. I also believe that it is not just the Hebrew God, but it is *Asha* the second member of the divine triad of the Gathas."

Caspar watched as the eyes of some of the priests grew wider. *Could it be?*

His father continued, "Melchior has asked us to make ready for a journey. He says this one who is the new king was born in a place outside of Parthia."

"Where? Where is this king and why would he not come to Parthia?"

"I do not know where he is, but Melchior is planning to go, and I think we should go with him."

"He could lead us into danger, to Egypt or to Rome! It is a trick Mithradata!"

A quiet voice cut through the argument, "Are you going?" Vishtat asked. Vishtat was a man of reason, respected by all.

Mithradata was very powerful. He was the link between the Parthian government and their sect of magi. The magistrate was divided into an upper and lower house. The upper house was formed by the nobles and the lower by the magi. Within the magi there were different sects, though this was not commonly known. Not all followed the same god or gods. Some had no god at all. Mithradata was a noble, but still a magus by practice. He was counselor to Phraates and his father before him. This was no easy task, and the king rarely listened to him, still it was a position of honor and the men in the room listened intently to his words as they always did.

There was a silence that filled the room. Though it was only a few seconds, it felt like an eternity.

"I believe in this journey, but my duties to King Phraates will not allow my travel. As you know, the king has not shown tact or prudence in regards to his family. I have tried to be the voice of reason, but still he has slaughtered so many of his family. He is suspicious these days. If he feels we are going to crown a new king, who knows what he may do."

The room was quiet. Phraates could kill them all if he found out they were leaving, or even speaking about a new king. Some voiced their protests:

"He might kill us."

"Then why risk a journey at all?"

"Phraates will see us leaving!"

"Yes," Mithradata had thought of that, "He will. I will tell him that there is no reason to be concerned. That you are going on a pilgrimage to see a prophet, then he will not bother you."

Caspar caught his father's eye. He knew what the look meant: he was asking him to lead his people.

"I will go," Caspar volunteered, knowing that he was volunteering to lead the Zoroastrians.

He believed it was his duty for, as his father liked to remind him, "someday he would represent the magi before the king".

"We must bring him gifts fit for a king," Argian advised, nodding his head. The old magus spoke, giving his approval to the journey and Caspar's leadership.

Another senior member of the group who had remained silent until this point spoke, "We are seekers of the light. If you say that a light in the sky has given you a sign and if you think he is the one we have waited for, what choice do we have? If we believe, then we must go on the journey. It may be that the light of truth is in this sign that has appeared in the skies, or it may be that it is only a shadow of the light. But how can we stay in the safety of our homes when something greater may wait for us? There is hope offered in this, and how can we not go?" He sighed, "I am too old for the journey. My days here are not long, but I will sell what I have and send it with you. Caspar, bring this new king of light my gifts."

Some of the others still looked doubtful, but they remained silent after hearing the two elders speak. They had come to a decision. Caspar would go, joined by as many that felt like making the journey.

Caspar nodded and one by one they went out of the room, some pledging to go on the journey, others offering tribute and giving their regrets, while a few only gave excuses.

There was strangeness in the air that he had never felt before. It was as if a spark leapt out of the fire and ignited the hearts and minds of the men around him. It was the spark of possibility.

"Thank you Caspar," his father addressed him. "I want you to go for two reasons: to see if this young king is the one for whom we have waited, and to protect our priests. They could be swayed to this Hebrew religion if they listen to Melchior. He is a most…persuasive man. I respect Melchior, but I don't want him to sway our people."

Caspar was silent. How could they be swayed? They knew the truth. Even if the prophecy was correct, it could not attach them to the Hebrew God.

MELCHIOR

The figure of Orion the Hunter slowly moved across the sky as slowly as a hunter stalking an elusive prey.

The old man, Melchior, watched as the stars in the sky danced. He watched Bethulah, the constellation of the Virgin. What he saw in the sky was not just a sign, but *the* sign. On this very day the sun, Shemesh, clothed Bethulah.

Yerach, the moon, stood under her feet. Though he knew the time by his counting, the sky messages still made his heart beat quickly. He had waited his whole life for these days.

There had been many wonders but this meant that he had come! *He had come!*

Melchior called himself a magus, but more than that, he considered himself a Jew. He believed that some of the magi were remnants of the lost tribes of Israel. He believed that is why Daniel, having no children of his own had chosen them, the descendants of the Medes. He had always thought of himself and the others who were entrusted with the prophecy to be descendants of the priestly tribe of Levi. The sect that had the special honor of carrying the prophecy was a small one.

Generation upon generation had waited and he was the one to be blessed. The parade of sights in the heavens foretold a momentous event. "A Messiah, a deliverer, will be born through the Jews, and his coming will bless all the nations," his father had taught. Melchior took the place of his father and his father before him. Each carefully memorized the words of the prophecy as a young man, and then as he aged, carefully taught it to his oldest son and successor. Not a word was to be forgotten or changed. This was their sacred duty.

Believing that the old prophecy, "The star will arise out of Jacob" had come to pass, he was ready to meet the new heaven-sent king. Praising the God of Abraham, Isaac and Jacob in his heart, he sat beneath the window for many hours lost in contemplation. He had been waiting for almost fifty years.

"Know therefore and understand, that from the going forth of the commandment to restore and to build Jerusalem unto the Messiah the Prince shall be seven weeks, and three-score and two weeks: the street shall be built again, and the wall, even in troublous times."

He recounted the words in his head. It had been forty-nine years since the order to rebuild the temple had been given. Even in Parthia, he had heard of the great task that had been undertaken. Now it was time.

"Grandfather, it's time to go to bed." A gentle voice shook him from his reverie. It was his Esther, his granddaughter and all the earthly family that had remained. She was beautiful, her long dark hair cascaded below her shoulders and her eyes shone as bright as the stars he watched in the sky. Daily, he would thank the Lord for her and asked him to bring her someone worthy to protect and love her. She was a dear girl, with a pure heart. He often wondered what kind of a man she should marry. An arrangement could be made, but no one had asked for her hand. Long ago, they had decided that she would have to love the man with whom she would be joined. How could he want anything less for the dear girl?

"I can sleep later. I have waited my whole life for this night!"

"Tonight grandfather?" her voice shook with anticipation. "Then He is here?"

"Yes child, he has come!"

They both laughed and danced. *He had come!*

Esther rejoiced with her grandfather. She too had been waiting for this moment her entire life. The two of them danced as they celebrated the moment.

They were the only family each other had. Finally, the worry of the last few years had lifted. Melchior wondered who would carry on the prophecy if he was to die. There were others in their sect, but still, there would have been no one to remember for his family. He wondered if Tigranes even remembered.

Esther was a baby when Tigranes left. Perhaps she reminded him too much of her mother who had died in childbirth. Melchior's dear wife had also passed away when the girl was very young and so the old man raised her as if she were his own.

He felt pain as he thought about his son, Tigranes. That night, as he closed his eyes, he heard voices and, as he drifted off to sleep, he remembered. How many years since Melchior had thought of his son? He had assumed he was dead, his dry bones forgotten somewhere, covered with desert sand.

Melchior's dreams were haunted with the memory of his wife anguished weeping as she held her son who was dressed for battle. "If this is what you must do. Go. May the Lord preserve him! May the Lord be merciful!"

As he slept he saw Tigranes, the defiant look in his eye. He had chosen to fight for Parthia. Melchior had wanted to give him words of strength and comfort, but he could not understand. He had been given a heavenly command, an ancient duty. How could he have chosen the worldly battle of a half-mad king?

Though he tried to hide his disappointment, he could not. Tigranes had rejected the magi, his duty and his God. He lumped the God of Israel with all the other gods---the god of the Zoroastrians, the gods of the Parthians, Greeks and Romans.

"How could there be so many? How could everyone be correct?" Tigranes had asked.

"Not everyone is correct," Melchior had answered, "there is only one God."

That day he embraced his son for the last time. Tigranes went to fight and never returned home.

THE MEETING

Bardan had asked to go with him, so he had allowed him to come. Balthazar looked at the young magus curiously when he had asked, but agreed to let him go. The young magus continued to puzzle him. Why would he want to go to Melchior's house? He was not known as a great entertainer. There would be no lavish feasts or dancing women. No, he was known as a simple man.

Melchior was a legend among the magi. Few knew him well, but all had great respect for the old man. He had helped many no matter what their sect with sage advice and even with gold when they were in need. He spoke plainly, his thoughts with no hidden agenda. Still, it was known to some that he worshiped the God of the Jews. Balthazar, who was usually the last to know about things, had heard that Melchior had been calling influential people to his house for "meetings." If that was the case, why was he called? He had no influence over anyone, *with perhaps the exception of Bardan.*

Balthazar went to the door and knocked. The door was

opened by a servant who invited them inside the large house. It was the house of a nobleman, though not too ostentatious. He noticed that there were no statues of the king or of any gods adorning the walls.

Almost immediately, a young girl came to greet them. She was young and lovely. Bowing her head in deference as she greeted them, she spoke, "Hello, my name is Esther. Thank you so much for coming. We are honored."

Balthazar greeted her, but Bardan remained uncharacter-istically silent. "I am Balthazar and this is Bardan, your… father…called for us."

She laughed, "He is my grandfather." She asked them to sit and promptly excused herself.

Melchior soon entered the room. "Welcome, welcome my friends! We have much to discuss."

As soon as they sat down, he began to speak. The old ma-gus explained that he had been meeting with different magi, trying to convince them to come with him on a journey. Some were interested, some even believed, but a trip of that mag-nitude would take a great deal of planning and expense. Who knew how far they would have to travel? Even his support-ers wanted to discuss matters further. Only the magi from his sect were eager and ready to go. As the day passed Melchior grew more frustrated and now he sat before a skeptic, trying to convince him to go see the Messiah.

Balthazar watched as the old man spoke of the prophecy. He had never heard of this prophecy, but he was describing the events that Balthazar had seen. It made him uncomfort-able, but did not convince him of anything. *Could this be a trick?* If so, trickery would not work with Balthazar. Still, Melchior was known for his straightforwardness. It would not be like him to use deception to further his cause.

As the men spoke, Esther brought them food and drink, then quietly left the room. She was welcome to stay, she knew, but she had heard this conversation numerous times during the last few months. Time after time her grandfather would receive a polite answer but no commitment from his followers. She knew this troubled him deeply but they had not discussed it.

Walking into the garden, she sat beneath a tree in the garden, her face buried in her arms. She believed in her grandfather's God. He was not just his God, but her God as well. She knew that her father had disappointed him. She was also disappointed. *Why wouldn't he want to carry on the ancient tradition?* How many nights had she prayed that he would return? She knew it was also the deep prayer of her grandfather, that and seeing the prophecy fulfilled. She believed in God's promise to care for those who put their faith in him.

The stories her grandfather told made her heart yearn for God. She longed for him as a thirsty horse pants for streams of water. Her deep thirst for the Lord frustrated her. How could she love the Lord God with all her heart, mind, soul, and strength if she was to be given to a man? How could she love God fully and still give proper honor to her husband?

And yet she understood the practicality of marriage. Though Parthian women had more rights than women in other lands, a husband could guarantee her security. Women were vulnerable and now, her grandfather was getting older. She had watched the other women, some her own age, swaddling their babies or running after their newborns. It was a deep desire of her heart to be a mother. Still, she believed there was more to marriage than security and children.

Perhaps it was a romantic notion, but whenever she heard her grandfather speak of her grandmother she knew that was what she wanted. Someone who loved her, *truly* loved her. Still, she wanted someone who loved God even *more*. That is what she most admired about the men in the stories her grandfather would tell. Their courage was impressive, but what made her heart beat was their conviction and bravery for God. She prayed, continuing to trust that the God who promised that they would send a promised one would also send her a husband.

She knew Bardan had noticed her. His face had become white when she entered the room, which made her feel good. She also knew that he did not love God.

They had hoped that this Messiah would be a mighty warrior that would help Israel rise up and join together again. Maybe he would have an answer. *But if he is a child now, how old would I be when he is old enough to rule?*

* * *

"Balthazar, I know you are a sky-watcher".

This was a fact. Everyone in the magistrate knew that he was a sky watcher.

"Let me tell you what you have seen." He went on to describe in detail what he, himself had seen in the last few months. Balthazar was astounded though he didn't appear so. He was describing the things he had kept hidden. *How did this old man know so much?* After he had described the occurrences he asked, "Is this what you have seen?"

"I…I do not call the stars by the same names."

Melchior pressed, "But have you seen what I have seen?"

There was nothing else to say but, "Yes, how did you know?"

"My whole life I have known when these signs would appear in the sky. I remember as a child my father looking at me with joy, telling me that if I lived to an old age I would behold the wonders foretold."

Bardan had not uttered a single word on this situation. This man believed the movement of the stars meant something supernatural.

"Why did you ask me here?" Balthazar asked coolly.

"I need your help."

"What kind of help can I offer?"

"I need you to speak with the people to tell them what I am saying is true. That you too saw these signs in the sky that the Messiah has come. The prophecy that said 'A Star will come out of Jacob, A Scepter out of Israel.' That time is now."

"I will not say that what I have seen in the sky means what you say, I do not know that they mean anything at all. Sometimes they predict changes in the weather, but a *Messiah...*"

"How can you question? Do you wonder how I know all that I have told you?"

"I do wonder, but it does not mean that any prophecy is correct."

Melchior looked astounded. He stared at Balthazar not knowing what to say. Internally he prayed, with all his might to God. He needed the support of this man. If he could get more support, then he would not have to make the trip alone.

"I need to go." He said quietly.

"Go where?" Balthazar asked, not sure what he meant.

"I need to go where the star leads."

Balthazar was astonished. First, he did not realize that Melchior was serious. He believed that the stars had a message to communicate to him, and that they were leading him to an actual location.

"Balthazar, you are a man of reason. Your mind is inquisitive. Don't you wonder at all if the stars could somehow tell you something? I cannot believe that you have not, just once, looked up and wondered if there was any meaning behind the celestial wonders you behold? Isn't there the smallest part of you that is curious my friend?"

"I know they mean something."

"You have dedicated your whole life to watching the stars. You know them, better than anyone I know. Didn't you ever wonder, or even hope that there was more of a meaning behind their movements?"

It was the last argument of an old man that made him think. He would never have admitted the fact, but there had been times when he had hoped. He watched the stars dance every night, every night for so many years. There were nights when he was alone and gazed up into the deep black of the sky that he would wonder if there was more. Those nights, he would hope that there was a great message. Balthazar was intrigued. The old man was so passionate about the journey. Still, it was not enough. He was uncomfortable now and did not want to listen to anything else.

"I will take your words under consideration," he said as they stood up to leave.

"Thank you," Melchior said. Then the men thanked the old man for his hospitality and they left.

Esther came in the room to find her grandfather on his knees, praying.

"What has happened?" she asked him cautiously.

"He will not go." Melchior answered in a heartbroken voice.

Esther could see the anguish in his eyes. To be so close was agony. "It doesn't matter, we will find someone else."

"I do not know, I thought they would listen to him. He was my last hope."

* * *

The marketplace had all the best Parthia had to offer. Esther had heard it said that the Parthian marketplace was unrivaled in the entire world. It beckoned visitors from regions near and far. Located along the trading route that followed the silk road, some vendors would have fine silks and cloths to offer. The fragrant spices that wafted through the crowded streets were from far-off lands. She could imagine nowhere else on earth as magnificent as the marketplace in Parthia. There were vendors selling exotic guavas, bananas, limes, figs, raisins, and pomegranates. The spice sellers offered cinnamon, vanilla, anise, and cloves. Sugar and honey were sold in booths as well. Jewels and metals were offered at other booths.

The food was always Esther's favorite part. She would

buy a few sweets drizzled with honey and her favorite: almonds! She would slowly eat them as she watched the people. People would push and shove, giving ample opportunity for those with a cunning heart and a quick hand. Too often she had observed small children getting pulled away from a booth after getting caught stealing.

Though they had a cook that would do most of the shopping, Esther still came to the market to observe. Closing her eyes, she would let the smells take her imagination to far-off lands. What place could produce such a fragrance? Her ears would focus on a foreign tongue, music of a world she did not recognize. How she wished she could visit every place and taste every food. For now, she would have to rely on her imagination.

Esther had asked where Bardan usually spent his time when he was not at the temple. She was told that he went into the marketplace on this day at this time to gather items for his potions. He was a man of habit, and she was thankful for that. Today she was wearing one of her best dresses as she shopped in the marketplace. Many a man had told her that she was beautiful, but she never encouraged their speech. Her heart twisted as she came up with her plan, but she needed this for grandfather.

He entered the marketplace as they said he would. Waiting, she hoping that he would see her and come speak with her. Within a few moments, he saw her. She smiled, and he smiled back. The crowd moved like the waters pushing the two of them closer. If they had not wanted it to be so, perhaps the current would have pushed them in another direction, but both of them had the same intention.

"Hello Bardan," Esther said when he was within earshot.

"Hello, Esther." He said nervously, looking quickly at the ground out of nervousness. The color of her clothing made her dark brown eyes sparkle.

"I did not get to tell you good-bye last evening. Thank you for coming." She started to move through the market slowly, and he followed, "It meant a lot to grandfather."

"Yes," Bardan said awkwardly. He wondered if she knew how the night had ended. Perhaps the old man had not yet told her.

"It means so much to both of us. Do you know if Balthazar has given the matter any thought?"

"I'm not sure if he has..."

She did not know what to say. By this time they had walked out to the furthest edges of the market place and were walking down the road together. Esther had never been one for pretense so she took a deep breath and began, "I don't think Balthazar was planning on going on the trip, but it means so much to us. We need others to go with us. My grandfather is too old to make the journey alone. It is much too long and dangerous. Would you please speak with him? Convince him to go?"

Bardan looked at Esther's pleading eyes. This strong and determined woman was asking for his help.

"You cannot go with him."

"Of course I can!" She snapped, "I too have been waiting for the Messiah."

The Messiah? Who was the Messiah? Bardan wondered.

Melchior had used the same word the night before, but it had not caught his attention.

"Esther, I do not know if Balthazar will go."

She looked down on the ground and saw a small flower struggling to rise above the grass. Her confidence never came from expensive adornments or even compliments. They came from the simple things.

"If you ask him, I know he will come," she asserted confidently.

"But I do not believe in your God."

"I know," she said.

But it will be a long journey and I will pray, she thought.

He looked at her once again and relented, "I will speak with him."

"Thank you, thank you Bardan!"
He smiled.

The Journey of the Magi

THE COUNCIL

"But it would be interesting!" Bardan had been trying to convince Balthazar to go on the journey for hours.

"No, absolutely not! I do not have any time!"

"Of course you do!"

Why he was pleading with him? It was useless but Bardan kept persisting. *Why does he want to go?*

Bardan kept watching the magus for signs of relenting. There were no such signs. *Think Bardan, think!* What would appeal to Balthazar?

"Melchior has called a meeting of the magistrate today." It was true. Melchior had become frustrated with waiting and chose to call the magistrate together where he could speak to them as a whole.

"What?" this information caught Balthazar off guard. Why hadn't he heard about the meeting? Of course, he had not been out of the tower all day, reading and re-reading his sky charts. Melchior's words had bothered him so he was looking for a plausible explanation for the events of the last few months.

Balthazar started to worry for the old man. He knew how cruel the magistrate could be when they gathered as a group. Though he did not agree with Melchior, he admired his conviction. *They will ridicule him.* In a moment he was on his way out the door with Bardan following behind him.

***

Melchior felt smaller and weaker with each step he took toward the meeting place in the temple. Never had he felt such hesitation. This place knew him well, but this time it was different. The magistrate was assembling; he had brought them together. There was hostility in the air. By now they had all heard about his quest. Who had dared to claim that the Hebrew God was greater than theirs? He had never said that, but it was the inference. Still, how could it not be so? They had forgotten Daniel, they had forgotten so much. Now he, close to seventy years of age, was going to remind them.

He remembered the words. They had been ingrained into him as if they were written on his soul. Recounting the prophecy gave him strength. Then he prayed.

God be with me, Oh, Lord, I am but a man. I believe. I do! Rid me of my doubts!

The Rab Mag straightened and spoke, "Why have you gathered us here, Melchior?"

Melchior watched them assemble. *Why would they listen to him?* He was an old man asking them to go on an arduous journey. Never before had he seen so many people assembled. The noise was deafening, filling every bit of the space. People spoke with each other and he could just imagine what they were saying. Though they would never say it out of respect, some of the members thought he was crazy.

He had spoken to Mithradata and was happy that he had the support of the Zoroastrians. Would that be enough? Could they sway the others? Scanning the crowd, he did not see Mithradata among them.

If Balthazar had agreed to come, the others would surely have followed him. So many of the magi expressed interest but there were too many religious conflicts. Balthazar was a man who did not have a claimed religion or sect. He was an anomaly among the magi and that is why his decision would have held so much weight. Melchior's eyes scanned the crowd for the dark haired man.

Melchior would have to speak quickly. A crowd this large would not go unnoticed and though the Parthian kingdom had respected the magi, nothing could be left to chance.

Caspar also watched as the group assembled. Why was the old man doing this? His sect had traveled the trade routes, they could keep him company. They would slip away at night, there was no need to include the other magi. He made his way to the front of the crowd and stood near Melchior.

Balthazar made his way into the temple just as Melchior was about to begin. He could not stop him now, so he stayed in the back. Bardan made his way toward the front next to Esther. As Balthazar watched he realized why his young friend had tried so hard to convince him to reconsider.

As Melchior stood up the crowd quieted down. "I do not have much to say. You know that I am preparing to leave on a journey. Some of you know why, others have heard rumors. I believe that in the west, a new king has been born. I intend to go and visit him. I welcome you to do the same. We have waited for many years for this one to come. It will take time to prepare, but we must make haste. Months have passed while we have been discussing amongst ourselves. I intend to leave. Those who are willing to join me, make haste.

"What will happen when Phraates hears of this?" they murmured. "He will think we are going to crown a new king!"

Caspar stood up, speaking loudly, "I am Caspar, son of Mithradata. My father is counselor to the king. I do not deny that there is an element of danger to this trip, but I do not believe we will have to worry about Phraates. There are many Zoroastrians, including myself, who are making this journey. We do believe that there will be a royal child and we will go as a great convoy to meet this new king. It is the great tradition of the magi to welcome the new kings. Who will join us?"

Something about Caspar's enthusiasm prompted some of them to raise their hands and cheer.

An unknown force prompted Balthazar to speak. "I too will go!" He was on his feet before he could control himself, "who will join us?"

The room felt silent for a moment then suddenly hands were raised in every direction. There was a new excitement. Esther threw her arms around Bardan with pure joy. Melchior beamed. Balthazar was at a loss. *What had prompted him to speak?*

THE JOURNEY

Vithradata had come to Caspar, imploring him to leave immediately. Months had passed since Melchior held his meeting in the temple. Planning and preparations were underway, but no date of departure had been determined.

"If you are going to leave, now is the time." He told his son quietly.

"Has something changed, father?"

"No, but I believe it may quickly change. I fear the king's days are numbered."

"Do you suspect the prince?" It had become commonplace for the royal families to plot each other's death's in order to keep the throne.

"Maybe, but the queen is also acting suspiciously. If you do not leave now and something happens, then as the kingmakers, they will never let you go."

"Maybe we should stay. Wouldn't it be our duty to announce the next king?"

"No, you must go. You must see if this child is the one prophesized. If he is, then he is the answer."

Caspar nodded as anticipation mounted. He went to the Melchior under the cover of night and together they set the time for departure. Two days later the caravan was ready to depart.

***

Esther breathed in awe when she saw the size of the caravan. She could not see where it began or ended.

"Over ten thousand," she heard one man say.

"Almost twenty thousand," she overheard from another. It did not matter. Her heart beat with joy knowing that at last they would be making their journey. She had heard her grandfather say when the Hebrews were captured and taken to Babylon the sons of the tribes of Reuben, Simeon, Judah, Dan, Naphtali, Gad, Asher, Issachar, Zebulon, Joseph, Benjamin, and the tribe he claimed, Levi were among those taken. He had told her that they still had descendants in Parthia. She wondered how the ancient Hebrews left Egypt so quickly with such a large group.

It had taken them months to prepare. Melchior worked with each sect of magi to make provisions for their members. It was difficult attempting to tear a group of scholars and nobles from the comforts of their home, take them to unknown lands with unknown inhabitants, and lead it for three, six, twelve months in the desert. This group would inevitably face thirst, hunger, and the unknown. Melchior had warned them that it was very possible some of them would not come home. Such was the huge undertaking of Melchior.

Camels and horses were weighed down with large barrels of water and sacks of provisions. Other animals carried tribute the nobles wished to present to the new king. Hired Parthian soldiers flanked the caravan, protecting the nobles and their tribute. The soldiers went first then the nobles followed by the magi sects. The servants, cooks, and animals would follow and behind them another set of soldiers.

Mithradata had counseled the group to take advantage of a time when Phraates was distracted. If they were found out, it could have meant death for all of them. Phraates had was highly suspicious of those that would take his throne. He had killed many male relatives, including his own father and almost thirty brothers. It was not unusual for a Parthian king to kill family members who might take his throne, but Melchior had never seen a king kill so many.

Though the Parthians were not at war with any kingdom, they would face skirmishes from time to time. Mithradata worked within the palace walls to ensure that the king and queen had their attention diverted to one of those skirmishes. Thus the mass exodus occurred peacefully.

The caravan was so immense that the front of the caravan began moving hours before the end of the caravan. Some magi had on their finest robes and so a caravan of people, animals, and canopies of varying colors departed the great city.

The keepers of the secrets rode around Melchior. By now all the magi had heard of the prophecy, but they were the most excited, having waited the longest. Esther traveled with her grandfather. Bardan traveled with Balthazar, but close to Melchior's sect. Caspar also traveled closely. He did not forget his duty to his father to watch those that worshiped the Hebrew god.

As the sun set, Balthazar watched the rising of the King Planet. If it had been Melchior he would have said it was a divine force that was leading them leading to the new king.

Balthazar wondered how long this trip would take and where it would lead them. He worried what stood before them.

They sang songs as they departed. Melchior prayed as he began the journey. Now, finally, they would go to see the new king no longer a newborn but still a baby. Some men were obviously moved with excitement. They cried out:

"We are going to welcome the new king!"

"The prophecy has been fulfilled!"

"It will be a marvelous journey!"

I just hope that we make it back alive, Balthazar thought.

Melchior rode up to Balthazar.

"When the sun goes down and the stars appear, please direct us where we are to go. Your skills will be of great value on this journey, " he instructed.

Balthazar did not respond. Melchior waited a time then continued to speak, "Looking at the stars forces me to slow down, to look outside myself and my own problems. I concentrate not just on the creation but the creator. It brings me into contact with God. Every star has a story of birth, and even death. It requires us to take from it the entire story it contains, learning from its meaning. When the prophecy was given, it contained the soul of Daniel, the man who served as God's instrument to protect this prophecy through time. God uses us in different ways, the sky-watcher, the weaver, the potter. We all place our soul into our work. We all search for meaning in the everyday, because there is meaning. Balthazar, you watch the stars you know and understand but there is a greater meaning to what you do. That is why I believe God has chosen you."

Balthazar nodded, not wanting the old magus to continue his monologue. He was uncomfortable and angry. *Why was he the one to lead them?* It was not to be Melchior or even the Zoroastrian magi Caspar. No, he was the one that would have to lead them to their god.

These men had followers, but he was the one that would lead. Balthazar had brought his charts with him, but wondered if this was a foolish journey. He, more than any other, knew the predictability of the stars. They, however, were relying on the first anomaly he had seen since he was a young boy, walking with his father in the temple. They were relying on the unpredictable and unprecedented. It made him more than nervous. The responsibility was great. What would they say if the journey was not successful? Who would they blame then?

Caspar rode close to Argian. The old man had insisted on coming along. He was at least fifteen years older than Melchior who, in Caspar's opinion, also seemed too old for the journey.

Some nobles rode on horses using their camels to carry their supplies, and still others were carried in seats swung between two mules. Argian, however, chose to walk. He was dressed in immaculate white linen over which a second garment of white wool was thrown. He wore no jewelry while the other Zoroastrian priests were adorned with necklaces, collars, armlets, and anklets of gold set with precious stones. Their head-dress was cap-like, with a circular curtain which falls over their shoulders to protect from the great heat of the desert. As was their practice, their dress was clean and light. Some of the men wore an added tunic of a different texture and pattern, reaching to the thigh. This was clasped on the shoulder, and held in place at the waist by a girdle. Argian wore his tunic in the style of the older men with a long mantle which was bordered by a distinct fringe, sewed to the edge of the material.

Some of the magi wore dazzling robes of different colors. There were a few that carried long wands while others wore masks of varying designs. Those that were influenced by the Egyptians wore masks in the shape of the sacred ibis, hawk, bull, and ram. Many wore cylindrical caps, wider at the top than the bottom, with a diadem surrounding the crown or decorated with different emblematic ornaments.

The group contained a few women who wore bright colored garments that reached to the ground. They too covered their head with headdresses and scarves.

As they moved some sang while others played music.

As Caspar walked, he heard one of the nobles singing:

You, who have dreamed, know that they are now true.

To follow the dream, that is to you,

If you have the soul and the Spirit,

Do not fear, you will know what to do.

Hearts can inspire, other hearts come with fire,

For the strong obey when The Lord shows them the way.

Come now, all men, all the noble, learned men,

Who will fight, for the God they adore,

Start me with ten, faithful and strong men,

And I'll soon give you ten thousand more.

Shoulder to shoulder and the young and the older,

Will grow as they go to the fore.

We will go as a force, with breath and with speed,

To see the one who is destined to lead.

When convicted men can stick together man to man.

***

They traveled for several days and the caravan was filled with sounds of jubilation. They would wake early and travel until mid-day. This is when they would rest. Again, they would walk in the early evening when it became cool and camp again deep into the night. Traveling at night allowed Balthazar to best determine their route.

Esther hummed a song to herself as she walked. Bardan walked next to her.

"What is that song?" Bardan asked.

"It is the song of praise to God."

Bardan was silent as he walked. Esther loved her God. Would she love someone who did not follow him? There had been moments when he had even considered a love spell, but he dismissed the thought. For some reason, he wanted her to love him of her own accord. Several nights they spoke of the things of nature. She had even told him of her father, though there was little to tell.

"He went to battle."

"You never saw him again?"

"No, but sometimes when the world is silent I try to imagine him, remember the sound of his voice. I do not have any memories of my mother, but I have some of my father. I wonder if he is alive sometimes. Grandfather raised me. I know he misses him though he never talks about him."

She turned and looked at him. "Bardan, his face is filled with hope now." She grabbed his hands in thanksgiving. "I will never forget it was you that helped place it there."

THE ZAGROS
MOUNTAINS

The days grew shorter as they walked further away from the great city. Though some had traveled this route for trade, most had never ventured outside the city walls. Some still sang songs while others were beginning to grumble.

At first, Melchior ignored the complaints. Then the old man grew frustrated. Didn't they understand that *this* was the time for which their ancestors had waited? They would see what their forefathers only *dreamed* of seeing. *They* were the blessed ones.

"This is the end of your waiting! Rejoice! We will lay eyes on he who has been promised!" he would remind them.

Those from his own sect were easily reminded. They too had kept the secret for generations. The Zoroastrians could be persuaded to keep their spirits high, but the nobles of the high magistrate grew weary easily. Grumbling loudly, they began to try and use their magic to speed up the journey and make predictions about their arrival.

The group came to the foot of the Zagros Mountains. Crossing these mountains would be extremely difficult. These mountains climbed higher than any in the area. The paths would be unpredictable and very dangerous.

Caspar watched Argian with nervous anticipation. How was the old man going to make this trip? They began to climb, higher and higher, as one giant mass of people. The road grew steeper as they climbed. As the road became more narrow and steep, even Balthazar began to worry.

What lay before them was over two hundred miles of almost impassable mountains to cross. Thankfully, few in the caravan knew this fact. There was no turning back in the middle of the mountain pass, not with this many people. From here, they would have to go forward.

Zagros was savage and wild. It would be nearly impossible to move through the untamed mountains. The mountains reached high into the sky, winding along river beds, threading between jagged pinnacles and ravines. In places, there was little more than a footpath. In some places, they would have to travel one by one---one man and one animal at time and there were thousands of them.

They walked several hours until they found a place where they could rest. A few soldiers were then interspersed throughout the group. This way, they could help those who needed help and relay messages quickly. In the mountains they would have to prepare against the elements, not an unknown army. The road was not always clear or ready to handle a group of that magnitude. The soldiers had been given groups to oversee. If a road crumbled before them, they were instructed to take another route, finding one if necessary. They hoped that they could all meet at the bottom of the mountain if anyone had to take an alternate route. No one wanted to get separated from the group, however. The mountain range was so large that if they got separated it was doubtful that they would ever see each other, or anyone else, again.

Resting where and when they could, they pushed forward. The air grew thinner as they climbed. It became more difficult to walk long distances, especially for the older magi. As they moved, they covered their faces shielding themselves from the wind and cold.

Every night the magi would gather with a like-minded group and pray, conjure or speculate. In the last few days the group had grown even quieter, preserving their energy as they walked. Even though he was a man of quiet, even Balthazar longed for a group to sing or even to speak. The silence drew him within himself, maybe it was the same for everyone.

There was no way to go but forward. Once they entered the mountains, Balthazar did not have to set the day's route, but he still worried about what they would find beyond the mountains. The mountains themselves were extremely dangerous. They had to watch carefully. Daily, a valued item or an animal would fall off the edge into the abyss.

Balthazar had walked alone these last few days. Bardan spent most of his time walking with Esther. The young magus preferred the company of Melchior's daughter to his own. This was a relief most of the time, but in rare moments Bardan would still walk with him.

"It is glorious, isn't it? Beautiful!"

Balthazar followed Barden's gaze. They stood at the edge of a cliff. There was no end to the untouched mountains in sight. The mountains were seamless, one moving into another with fluidity as if it was planned by an unknown force. The beauty was so overwhelming that it caused Balthazar's heart to ache. He could not explain it, and would not even try. Even though he was looking out, in that moment made him remember all these things he had forgotten. *Strange*, he muttered to himself.

"But Balthazar, isn't it beautiful?" Bardan persisted.

"Yes," he sighed, the beauty of the mountains was not debatable.

As they continued through the mountains, Balthazar's

thoughts returned again and again to his father. *The old man would have loved this journey.*

"Walk toward the unknown. That is where you will find yourself," his father would say.

Perhaps we would have been forced to talk, Balthazar reflected.

His thoughts drifted from his father to Melchior. Strangely, the old man reminded him of his father. It was more than their age. They both were passionate about the things they loved, and what they loved was the intangible. His father, however, would move from idea to idea. Melchior, on the other hand, remained loyal to his beliefs.

The Zoroastrians carried lamps on the journey. Constantly, someone kept the fire going. The others whispered that they worshiped the fire. This was not the case. No, they used the fire as inspiration and protection. It would keep them safe during the journey.

When he was in doubt he would look to the fire, remembering the Good Spirit. The ancient tradition calmed him, focused him and allowed his mind to journey. As the flames danced he would be soothed from the worries of the day and be reminded that there was a purpose in everything he did. The fire, when pure, could inspire men to great things. It would draw stories from their heart. How many nights had he listed to men speak around the fires in the temples?

Though they did not have the temple fire, Caspar found solace in the surrounding beauty. The mountains gave him time to contemplate the gravity of what was before him. The quiet was like a warm blanket to him. What would his father be doing at this moment? He would be speaking with some high-ranking official about the sacred texts or the political climate of Parthia. He, though, was a man of introspection, searching for meaning in every moment.

"Why do you carry this light my friend?" Melchior asked.

"It shines in the darkness. The purpose of light is to create more light."

"For what are you searching, Caspar?" Melchior asked.

Caspar was taken aback by the question. He looked into the eyes of the older man and it was as if he had never seen him before. What did he want?

"Searching? I don't know that I am searching for anything."

"Everyone who has come on this journey is looking for something. Even Balthazar is searching for something, though he would not admit this to be true."

The question made him uncomfortable. Was this old magus trying to convert him to worship his God? He knew why he was on this journey. He went because he was expected to go. As quickly as he had come, he rode away again.

What was he hoping to find?

* * *

Argian gasped for breath as he continued to walk. The higher elevation was making it painful to breathe. The wind ripped through his body as he took every step. Perhaps this was not the journey for a man of his age, but he had to continue. He did not complain, but pushed himself forward, counting the steps and praying as he climbed. The Zoroastrians were excited at the possibility of seeing the prophecy fulfilled but still, they were unsure about following a man as young as Caspar. Argian spoke in his defense, calming the fears of the others because of his age and wisdom. He had to come and knew at the start of the journey that he most likely would not make it to the end.

Every night he would find Caspar and talk to him about the things of life, imparting to him every word of wisdom he could give. Argian knew his father, Mithradata well, but he was a man who liked things to stay unchanged. He was faithful of course, that is why he supported the journey.

As the nights passed, Argian learned more about Mithradata's son Caspar. This young man was a leader, though he did not yet have confidence in his abilities. Argian also noticed that Caspar had a thirst for knowledge and truth unlike his father. He watched as Caspar listened with respect when Melchior spoke of his God.

One night, Melchior spoke to the both of them about his hope for the new king, "The Messiah" he would call him.

"We call him Messiah because he will deliver the Jewish people from their captors."

"So all the people of Israelites will be united?" Caspar asked thoughtfully.

"That is my hope," Melchior nodded. He had imagined it many times over the years. A great warrior, the messiah would arrive. The sleeping tribes of Israel would unite against all their enemies and the Jewish people would rule over all those who had conquered them over time.

"Then why did you invite us on this journey Melchior?" Caspar asked him.

Argian smiled to himself. Amused that the young man would ask such a direct question, but interested to hear the answer.

Melchior thoughtfully spoke, "I did not grow up in the land of my Israelite ancestors. Truth be told, not all of my ancestors were Israelites. I can trace my family line back to the time of the Rab Mag, but then my ancestors were Medes. Some say that we are descendants from the ancient tribe of Levi, but these are stories. I believe that there are descendants from the lost tribes of Israel that make this pilgrimage with us. Still, time has passed and we cannot be certain."

"Then why do you go?" Caspar persisted.

"I believe the one who has been born is a king for all the nations. Why would Daniel have trusted us with the prophecy if God did not want it to be so? He is king of all people. I think he has come to unite the Israelites, yes. I also believe that he has come for a bigger purpose than that. Whatever it is Caspar, it involves you and me and all the magi that have come in…in faith."

"Beautiful words my friend." Argian replied.

"Do you believe my words?" Melchior asked.

"I do not know what we will find. Some of the ancient stories say that Zoroaster was a pupil of Daniel, who had been taken captive when Nebuchadnezzar made his first expedition against Jerusalem. His prophecies, as well as aspects of the Hebrew Scriptures, and some of Daniel's own private comments, came to be included in our Zend Avesta. It contains a prophecy that says there would be born unto us a king, and that his coming would be heralded by a sign in the heavens. That is why we have come. It is all because of the prophecies of the same man, so many years ago.

"I hope they are true," Caspar remarked.

"We all do," Argian pointed out, "and if they are, I believe it will be a glorious thing."

* * *

The front of the caravan had gotten word that two nobles and a servant had fallen off the side of the mountain that day. Soldiers had come bearing the news to those before and behind them. Now that death had visited them, the whole group had grew even more anxious.

"Some want to go back," Barden commented to Esther as they walked.

"That is foolish," she retorted. She would not admit it to him, but she too was nervous. They all knew that they could die on the journey, but it didn't feel like a real possibility until now.

"We've been walking for weeks now, of course people will be afraid," Barden observed.

"Yes, but the mountain is unpredictable, you've seen that." He had. He had seen walkways washed away. Some had started throwing items that were too heavy or troublesome to carry off the side of the mountains. They had even come across places where the road had been worn away and they had to leap slightly to get to footing. Thankfully they were small breaks in footing, but it had been a struggle to get some of the animals across.

"Their families won't know for a long time"

"Probably not," he agreed, "unless someone sends them a dream."

"A dream?"

"Yes, I've heard some of the sorcerers can send dreams. Kings have used these dreams to send words in battles."

She was quiet. The idea of sorcerers conjuring dreams disturbed her. She believed God spoke in dreams. God spoke through Nebuchadnezzar and Daniel. Bardan acted as if it was commonplace to do such a thing. Grandfather had always warned her to be wary of those magi that practiced the occult magic.

"Of course it would work; there is no power or danger in things that do not work. Just ask yourself when it does work, where does the power come from? If it does not come from the God of Abraham, Isaac and Jacob, from where does it come?"

The words echoed in her head as she walked.

***

Another week passed and they slowly began their descent. It was not as easy as Balthazar had thought. It was not as difficult as the ascent, but still would take work. Thankfully it became easier to breathe and warmer as they moved to lower elevation. The stars had continued to move and so he continued to lead them. He wondered how it would be in the flat land.

THE PLAINS

As he slept his dreams were filled with the same face that filled his days: Esther---mysterious, implacable Esther. As the days passed, his heart struggled vainly not to allow itself to fall in love with this woman who didn't belong to his world. His mind and heart battled for what seemed like years but in reality was a few seconds. His whole body cheered in those moments that reason lost the battle. All Bardan could do was surrender and accept that he was in love. But what did that mean? Marriage? He did not know Melchior well, but would the old man allow his only granddaughter to marry outside of his sect and beliefs? Would she even consider him? Especially since she brought him face to face with a God he did not understand or want to understand.

Weeks passed, they kept walking. Finally, they made their way down the mountain to the much awaited steppe land in the plains.

"Finally," many cried with relief. Though beautiful, the mountains journey had been difficult for many of them. Their feet ached and their bodies cried out for the comforts of their homes.

The plains were flat, yes, but as they looked before them they could see nothing, reminding them that the journey before them was most likely, much longer.

Esther lay in the grass, gazing up at the stars. Her grandfather saw so much up there, but all she saw was the beauty. Sometimes she could feel so small looking up at the sky, but then the words of her grandfather reminded her that she was created by a mighty God for a purpose.

She smiled when she thought of Bardan. He had been so kind. She noticed that his voice grew softer when he spoke to her and his eyes never left her face. *What are you doing God? Are you working on his heart?*

Bardan surely was working on hers, and it grew more difficult to protect. He was not a believer, but he was kind and attentive.

Please God, protect my heart. I give it first to you.

She turned the conversation to the new king.

"Tonight he's just a baby. Tonight he's sleeping beside his mother." She told him as they walked.

Bardan thought it was a curious thing. It was the truth. A child, they were going to pay tribute to a child. It seemed so ordinary. He would think that if he had waited hundreds of years for a God to appear he would do it in a more dramatic way. A baby seemed so…ordinary, so easy to overlook.

Why wouldn't he come with a legion of angels or in a chariot of fire?" Bardan asked, "He would be much more difficult to ignore."

Esther thought on this then replied, "Perhaps He does not just want our attention, but our love."

Love? What kind of a God wanted love? Power he would understand. Tribute and worship made sense, but love?

***

Bardan received word from a messenger that the sorceress Avashya wanted to meet with him. This was strange. It was not unusual for those who dealt in the occult arts to work together in collaboration or to consult each other. Together, their potions would be much more powerful. However, he never asked for her assistance. It was rumored that her power was great. Still, something unsettled him about her.

Passing through the crowds of people, he followed the messenger to her tent. Why would this woman want to speak to him? *Why she had come on this journey?*

Contrary to what the other magi thought, Bardan had power. He had predicted many things by looking into the leaves and his potions. He had foreseen Phraates killing his family and though he had told no one, he had even seen the queen plotting his death and sitting on the throne with her son. It had been disturbing indeed.

Bardan knew that there were some predictions better kept to himself. He had tried to think of a way to use this information to advance in the court of the king.

Avashya was powerful in her own right. He had heard many a local had gone to her for a fortune telling, a love potion or something similar. Most of the magi in the temple looked down on this lower magic. He wondered if some were threatened by the idea. Bardan did not like it because it was self-serving, there seem no nobility to her work. He had sought purpose in his efforts. That is why he wanted to learn from Balthazar.

When Bardan arrived at her tent, he found a small crowd around the old woman who was making a potion. He made his way to the front and asked, "Are you Avashya?"

The old woman spoke, nodding, "You know who I am."

He nodded his agreement then asked, "What do you want to say to me?"

The old woman thought a moment then said to the others, "Leave us now, we must speak". The others left the tent immediately on her command. After the others left she spoke with the young magus.

"I have seen things, and they are not good."

Wondering if she too had seen the death of the king, he asked, "Tell me what you have seen."

"It is not good at all," she continued not giving him any details.

"Speak directly to me, or I will leave. I do not have time for you," he said strongly.

"No, no you do not have any time for those of us who practice, You only have time for the magus Melchior's daughter."

He looked at her, angered. It was true, but who was she to know his business?

"What I have to say concerns you. Do you know where this trip will end?

"Of course I do. Do you know?"

"This will be our undoing." She said, shaking her head.

"What do you mean?"

"I know you Bardan. You seek power not knowing that you possess more than most. It is a power that you do not fan into flame, but still power. You have the ability to see. I too have that ability." She shook her head in sadness, "Today I wish I did not."

Uncomfortable, he let her continue speaking.

"I have seen what is at the end of this journey. I have seen the child."

Bardan waited, now captivated by her words. Where was this child? How much longer did they have to rave?

"This child will be our ruin Bardan," Avashya said, her voice cracking.

Our ruin? "What do you mean?"

"This is a child born to a virgin, from the house of David. I have heard that this is true. I have also seen the child as a man. His *death* will be our ruin."

His DEATH? "You are speaking of a child who is still an infant. He is alive. I do not understand what you mean."

Her eyes grew big as she spoke. "Bardan, this child will be our ruin. Our powers will be worthless. We will no longer have a place in the temple."

You have no place in the temple, he thought to himself.

"We will be forced into the streets and dark corners. I have seen it!"

It made little sense to him. He had never thought of the actual child at the end of the journey, but what child could pose a threat to him. Even if he was a king, he would concern himself with conquering kingdoms not worrying about a temple magus.

"What do you want me to do? He asked the sorceress. She had chosen him for a reason.

"You must stop him; somehow, you must stop him! I know you do not believe me. I know that you have the power to see. Ask for yourself. You can see and *know*."

She was so sure of herself. *Did he want to know?* If he looked and saw the future Avashya foretold, what would that demand of him? Shaken, Bardan moved out of her tent and found his way back to the nobles. What could this mean? He could pass it off as the ravings of a lunatic, but something gnawed at him. Her words could be true, and then what?

The Journey of the Magi

THE DESERT

The sun never seemed to set. It mocked them from the sky, draining all their energy. They had reached the desert, it was undeniable. The sun continually beat down upon them as they set up their camp. The large group trudged onward step by step. The group would rise just before dawn every morning and walk till mid-day. Then the caravan would rest till sunset and walk again for a few hours till late night. It was easier to walk and ride in the cool of the night, but difficult to sleep in the heat of the day.

Clouds of dust rose around them as they moved, chaffing the skin on their faces. The night air was cooler and the sky watchers could tell them where to travel. The more affluent nobles had large canopies of protection carried over them by servants to shield them from the sun.

Balthazar watched Melchior. He intrigued him. The old magus was never too far from his side. Every day, he would visit with the same questions about where they were going. Melchior never asked for the destination, just the route. He never questioned Balthazar's words and that angered the sky-watcher. *Why did he trust him so much?*

There was no doubt in the old man's mind that he was going to see. Melchior's eyes shone with determination and a faith Balthazar did not possess. Still, the old man had asked for his help. *Why?* Surely his God would have provided a guide for them, someone else to show them the direction of the star.

***

Melchior and Caspar sat by Argian's side. He had been well when they reached the desert, or so they thought. Then he had fallen gravely ill. For six nights now Caspar had kept the fire burning, never leaving his side.

"Do not look so sad my son; you know that I will see you again."

Caspar nodded. They, unlike so many of their contemporaries, believed in an afterlife. Melchior too had been spending a great deal of time in the old man's tent. The younger magus realized that the older magus had slowed down the entire caravan for this old man. For that he was grateful.

"Do not look so somber my friend!" Argian said to Melchior, "You must greet this king for the both of us."

"I will! And you, you believe that this life is not the end either. Perhaps I will see you again too."

"Perhaps."

"Yes, maybe I will finally meet your Abraham, Isaac and Moses…"

Melchior grabbed the other man's hand tightly. "I truly hope you do, friend."

Argian spoke, "Melchior, take care of this young one. Caspar, Melchior has wisdom to share. Trust him. I have tried to give you all that I know."

Caspar nodded, he was blinking away tears. This man had become closer to him than his own father.

"Your father chose the right man to lead. Do not doubt

yourself. I pray that my good deeds have outweighed the evils I have done. Now stay with me while I repent for all that I have done wrong."

Shortly after, Argian died.

***

It had been a week since Argian had died. A delegation of magi came to visit Caspar's tent as they camped. They were upset. Caspar had dreaded this moment, knowing that it was just a matter of time. He had heard some of the men grumbling. The leader of the group, Korah confronted him,

"Do you know where they are leading us?"

"We are following the directions in the night sky."

"That is foolish!" another magus spoke. "They must know where they are going! Melchior can be deceptive; you cannot believe what he says. He would have us all bow to the God of the Hebrews."

He looked at their faces; they were full of fear and anger. Why were they so threatened? Some now acted as if they did not want to see the child, that they did not want him to be *the* king. He saw distrust and secrecy grow within the members of his own sect. They still kept the sacred light burning to remind them that the light and that was always their goal. Truth would never bring more darkness.

"Caspar." Korah turned to him. "You should tell them which way we travel!"

He was immediately angered, "How could I do that? I do not watch the stars! I have come to know Balthazar. He knows the stars better than any man I know. What help could I offer him?

"It appears that the good spirit has chosen a man who does not worship any gods at all."

The delegation was taken aback, NO GODS. Even the Parthians believed in god. "The Good Spirit always goes before us and will lead us."

"Your father would not have allowed this to happen."

"Yes, Mithradata was a strong leader. He protected our people." Others lamented.

"My father followed the guidance of the light." He knew this was not always correct, but he knew his father tried.

"Would you want to wander in the desert? That is what would happen if I was to lead. I am your leader and as your leader I put my trust in Balthazar."

"We will accept Balthazar as a sky watcher, for now. But Caspar, you should ride by his side. Unlike some of these other magi, we have wives and children. Think of them. Encourage him to take the fastest route. Listen to him so you can advise him to go home if he loses the way. He does not believe in anything but himself!"

Caspar shook his head. "The good spirit will lead us. Light the fire, sing the chants. As we travel, look at the sky. Even I can see that there is something different in the night sky.

"Yes, we will but remember that your father chose you to lead us."

The words troubled Caspar. Some followed Zoroaster, others the Hebrew God and still others followed the gods of Babylon. Did his people want to divide them? But why was he so afraid? The truth could not divide. Argian had been able to get along with all of them. He had felt no threat from Melchior. He knew them, they had sat together, spoke together, even chanted in front of the fire. Wouldn't a united Parthia be better for all of them?

The delegation went away but even though they did this time Caspar worried that the next time would not be as easy.

OBSTACLES

The sorceress's words had stayed with Bardan. He had reviewed them over and over in his mind and it still bothered him. It had been tempting to see if her words were true and so he had sought answers.

Again, he pulled out a small bag containing his tools and began to chant. Lighting a fire he waited until the smoke appeared. It was where he found his answers. He conjured up his spirits and then asked again and again the same question. Who was this king? What would it mean for him? Again and again he received the same answer. This king would mean their destruction.

In the darkness of his tent, he continued to work through the night until exhaustion overcame him.

The next morning, he was quiet as they walked, still tired from the night. His practices took his concentration, and for one ritual, some of his blood. Esther came up beside him to walk. It was usual for her to seek him out but usually by this time of day, Bardan would be walking next to her.

Walking in silence for a few moments, she waited for him

to speak.

"How are you feeling today Bardan?" she asked.

"Not well," was all that he could mutter. He needed to think. For the first time since the start of the trip he did not want Esther by his side. She confused his thoughts.

"Can I get you some water?" she asked him.

"No" he said simply and so she said nothing, walking quietly next to him.

I know she is praying. She is always praying. This is my entire fault. If I had not convinced Balthazar to speak, we would not be here. I brought about my own ruin.

His mind raced as they walked. Then suddenly he walked ahead of her quickly, leaving her behind. She did not follow but fell behind.

Bardan was tortured. He loved her it was undeniable but still, he would not compromise.

***

What had happened? It had been eight days since they had spoken last. Why was Bardan acting strangely? Anger welled up inside her as she thought of him. Every day for months he had chosen to be by her side. She had told him story after story and had listened to him speak about his dreams. He wanted to have influence over the court, to do great things. He had dined with her and her grandfather. Now he was distant, refusing to speak with her.

As difficult as it had been to open her heart to him, she now would have to shut him out of her heart.

Night after night she continued to pray, but she would not go to him. No, God would have to bring him to her if that was what he had planned. Still, sadness hung over her as she thought of him. Melchior noticed the change in his grand-daughter. She had laughed often during the journey, now he had seen her crying when she thought he did not see. It was Bardan, this he knew.

The young man was kind, but Melchior still worried for Esther. He knew that Bardan practiced sorcery and claimed to believe in many gods, in every god. Melchior believed that he only truly believed in himself. This troubled the old man. Even if Esther had chosen a Zoroastrian, he would have understood, but a man who does not believe in anything aside from his own power concerned him. One night Esther had spoken to Melchior about Bardan.

"He thinks you are afraid of him," Esther revealed.

"Afraid?" the thought amused him.

"Yes, he says that you are afraid of those with power. That is why you do not discuss the matter with any of them. That you are afraid and so you do not want to understand.

Melchior thought about this. He knew that since the beginning of time there had been a battle between good and evil. Both sides had power he knew. To simply say, there was no power in magic would be naive. He had seen magi make things appear and disappear. He had even known some who had correctly predicted the future and create potions that brought about the desired results.

Melchior thought of those magicians that came before Pharaoh. When the God of Abraham, Isaac and Jacob worked through Moses turned the staff into a snake, all the court magicians could not undo God's power. He was amazed at how easily people are deceived

"What do you think Esther?" he asked quietly.

"That he is afraid," she answered.

"Of me?"

"That you are telling the truth."

Now he watched his granddaughter go through her day, with tears in her eyes. Esther was heartbroken, and her unhappiness pained him. *Dear Lord, do what is best for Esther. Give her peace.*

***

Korah still was not pleased with the events that were taking place. He had observed the young man speaking with Melchior several times. What would that mean for his people? They had been listening to the Hebrew stories. He knew some of the men were beginning to grow uneasy. They had traveled many miles through the mountains but now in the plains they had time to think. Some worried that they would never again see their home.

There were some that began to panic, worrying throughout the night so that they were of little use in the morning. He had tried several times to speak peace to these Zoroastrians but his words had little influence on them. Three times now he had gone to Caspar but little had been done. Caspar had come, met with the men and assured them, but still their cries came in the night.

Others complained saying that they were "too tired" to keep walking. They asked the others to carry their baggage, causing resentment to build.

Korah was a faithful follower of Zoroaster. He saw his people in pain and could stand it no longer; they had to return to Parthia. There was no plan and they would die. If Mithradata's son was unable to lead, he would. They would go in two days he decided and anyone was welcome to join them on the journey home.

He went to Caspar and told him his plan.

"Korah, you would have to go back through the mountains. It is dangerous."

"We will have to return that way later. This is less dangerous then what lies ahead."

"You do not know that."

"Neither do you, we know what lies behind us." His dark eyes met those of the younger man. Both were determined. Caspar could see that there was little he could do to convince the magus to stay.

"Why would you do this? What if Argian was here?"

"Argian is why we need to return! He did not have to die

out here! How can you watch your brothers suffer like this? While they cry in the night, you sleep. While they are weary in the day, you speak with the Hebrews and non-believers."

Caspar did not know what to do; he immediately went to Melchior for advice.

Melchior thought for a bit then spoke, "Let them go."

"What?" Caspar did not expect his answer.

"They did not have to come, it was their choice and if they decide to leave, it too is their choice." He turned to look at him, "but I truly doubt they will go."

He could not imagine anyone making such a long journey just to turn back. Even Balthazar, who had spoken about going back during the first few weeks of the journey, never spoke about it again after they reached the highest point of the mountains. No, they were trying to manipulate the young magus. It was a play for power.

Caspar went and found Korah and said, "Go, return with my blessing."

Korah was surprised, "Are you coming with us?"

Shaking his head he said, "No." He had a job to do and a journey to finish.

"What will your father say?" Korah asked.

What would he say? Caspar wondered. Would he be upset that they abandoned his only son in the desert, or happy that they refused to continue on a foolish mission?

"I do not know, but he wanted me to watch over our people. Many left, but some still stayed. I wish to go forward and seek what is ahead of me. If I did not, I would always wonder. I know that there are others who will feel the same way. They will stay and I will lead them."

The next morning a group of five hundred left the group. Caspar watched as Korah led the group back across the plains. Uttering a silent prayer he hoped that they would be safe and that his father would think kindly of him when he would hear Korah's report of how he sympathized with the others. Sitting on his horse he watched until they were out of sight.

"Why didn't you go with them?" a voice asked behind him.

He looked behind him. It was Balthazar.

"My destiny lies ahead of me. I have traveled this long, I will not give up."

Balthazar understood and nodded. He did not say anything, but that was the reason that he too decided to stay. It had been over a month, they had crossed over the most treacherous paths to come this far. Even with his doubts he could not turn back now without knowing what lay before them.

***

It was Melchior who suggested that they camp for three days.

Surprised, Esther asked, "Why would you want to stay grandfather?"

"I do not want to stay, but I think this is what is best for us. In prayer, I felt that this was the correct decision."

Esther nodded; she did not want to prolong the journey either. Now, more than ever, she wanted the journey to end. She had seen Bardan looking at her when he thought he did not notice him.

Why was he so silent?

That night her curiosity got the better of her. She walked to his campsite and found him staring up at the stars. Summoning her courage, she spoke. "I would like to speak with you."

He looked at her, surprised. Part of him wanted to walk away but he had ached to be in her presence. The fire made her face glow. Nodding she came closer.

"What have I done to you, Bardan?"

What had she done? Nothing. Nothing but love a God that threatened everything he knew.

"I'm not sure what to say…"

"Speak the truth, Bardan."

"It has been my mistake. Not yours. I should not have spent so much time with you."

His words hit her like daggers. She would not beg him to speak to her. No. She stood there for a moment, waiting for him to continue. He could not take the silence and continued to speak.

"I don't believe in your God, Esther." He said softly.

"I know that, Bardan."

"So it does me no good to speak with you."

"Does you no good? I do not understand." She couldn't understand why he was acting so strangely.

"Even if I wished to marry you, I could not."

Maybe this was true, but she had been hoping that some-how God would change his heart and that they could get mar-ried. "Because of my God."

"Yes."

"Bardan, you listened to me speak. You've listened to the others. Don't you believe that there is something greater?"

He had thought about this many times on the trip, but never before. If he chose to believe, what would that mean for him? He would have to change his ways. No one spoke. Finally, Esther broke the silence.

"I don't understand why we can't even be friends. You don't want to talk to me at all?"

She was too dangerous. He didn't just want to speak with her. Even looking at her made his heart pulse. There was nothing more he wanted to do than to take her in his arms, but she cost too much. It would mean everything had to change. He could have ignored her God before, but now…it was *different*.

"No, it would be a waste of my time." Turning away, he refused to make eye contact with her.

Tears were falling down her face by now. She would re-spect his wishes, even though she did not understand.

"I will respect your wishes Bardan and I will continue to pray for you."

She turned and walked away. Bardan sat by the fire until it died.

***

They camped for the night and rested the next day and night. Caspar prayed in front of the fire while Melchior prayed in his tent. On the morning of the third day a rider came to the caravan. He had pushed his horse, moving with great speed. It was a rider from the group.

"Wait! Oh thank the Great Being that I found you!" the rider said.

The five hundred who had left soon discovered that the path was even more difficult leaving as it was coming. They had no one to guide them. By the second morning, many had regretted their decision. On the second night Korah had called a meeting. They had decided to wait and send out riders to see if they could find a caravan and if they would be welcomed back.

"Yes, of course they can return." Caspar said.

"We will wait two days for them, tell them to hurry, we have lost a lot of time." Melchior added.

After the rider left, Caspar asked the old magus, "How did you know that they would return?"

"I did not, but I had a suspicion that they would continue to fight with you until they got what they wanted. Now that they have it and have found it distasteful, you will not hear them speak again of going home."

When Korah returned, Caspar welcomed him not saying a word about the error of this decision. He had instructed the others to be kind to those who had left, reminding them that it had been a difficult journey.

***

Balthazar went ahead to look at the sky. It was difficult in the day, but often when they stopped walking and set up camp he would ride out in the twilight. Sometimes he rode away to look at the stars, other times he rode to get away. Day and night the magi would come to him with questions. Not even the members of the magistrate, but servants of the upper house. They expected him to be a soothsayer. How long would it take? What lay ahead for them? How could he know? All he knew was that he was looking to see where the star was taking them, if anywhere.

He cleared his mind as he rode, closing his eyes as the wind blew in his face. Stopping, he looked at the sky. It was so vast and they were so miniscule. How long had this world existed? So many had been born and killed.

A rider came up upon him as he sat in the stillness. It was Caspar.

"Why do you keep following me, Caspar?"

He had noticed the man had been watching him closely for the past few days. It did not surprise him. It was no secret that many in the group thought he was working for one side or another. It had been a very lonely journey for him. Talking to one person for too long could arouse suspicion, so he had kept to himself.

The silence began to speak to him. At first, it fought him, bringing up the things he did not want to face. But now, he was strangely soothed by his companion silence.

"We both have the task of leading these people, Baltha-zar. Both of us have not wanted the duty, but it was given us."

"I certainly did not ask for this" he said bitterly.

"Yes, but if we do not stand together we will be divided. I know you can read the stars."

"I am not a prophet! If you want me to contrive some-thing, I cannot! I only know what I see."

"But doesn't what you see lead you to what you do not see?"

Balthazar did not understand. He just looked at Caspar,

waiting for him to continue.

Caspar looked at Balthazar for a long time, "You do not believe." No, he did not. He had spoken with Bardan these last few nights. They had lamented walking with the others. Balthazar began to feel more and more alone as Bardan spoke. He was not like him either. Bardan was trying to protect something.

"I believe in what I see," Balthazar commented.

"When you see the stars, do you wonder how they came to be?"

"Of course I wonder, but that does not mean I make up a deity to explain their origin."

Caspar wondered if the God of Light had brought the two of them together "I don't want to follow the ways of others just because of tradition."

The younger man nodded, knowing there was something else bothering Balthazar.

"What is worrying you?"

"That these people are looking to me to lead them."

"Yes, that worries me too. We've been walking for so long now and we're running out of water.

Balthazar had noticed, everyone had noticed. There was no water. What they had brought with them from the last water they had seen was almost gone. There were no springs in sight at which to quench their growing thirst. The animals too were growing thirsty. The people began to grumble. The travelers struggled against exhaustion. Their animals now struggled under the weight of their possessions. Even those who believed as Melchior were getting nervous.

"What are we going to do?"

"We have to meet with Melchior."

The next day the three men met to discuss the situation.

"We need water, Melchior." Balthazar repeatedly said.

Melchior knew this, but he continued to rely on his faith.

Balthazar was gravely concerned. They had not faced a situation as dire as this. "We don't have enough water to turn back."

"If we turn back we still will not have water. We know what is behind us, but we do not know what is ahead. The Lord is leading us, Balthazar."

"To our death? I can follow the stars, but the stars will not lead us to water."

"The people are growing restless. Many have run out of water. Some are hiding water. If we do not find any, the people will start to fight amongst themselves." Caspar observed. He also was trying to trust, but he believed the situation demanded action.

"Our journey could not be much longer," Melchior countered.

"We'll be dead of thirst long before we get there!" Balthazar grew angry as he spoke. Melchior was not listening.

"The Lord will provide what we need," the old magus continued to say.

Balthazar tried to contain his anger. There was no talking with Melchior. The old man was single minded. He did not care that person after person visited his tent in the heat of the day begging him to find water. They were tired, thirsty, whining and complaining.

"When will we get there?" they asked him over and over.

Caspar could not think of a solution. He had seen some grow sick because of the heat. Some travelers had rashes on their skin. "We need water!" they would tell him. He knew. He needed water too.

"We have no water to give you. No one has." He would say.

"What are we going to drink? We will die without water"

Melchior remained calm when they asked saying, "The Lord will provide what we need."

Balthazar only heard the complaints of the others:

"When? We need water *now*!"

"There is no water here!"

"How long will this journey last!?"

"Why do we listen to these men? We have done nothing but suffer since we left Parthia!"

Silently, Melchior prayed. *Do not let us die on this journey.*

Desperate, Balthazar and Caspar rode out ahead of the caravan night after night to look for water in the deep hours of the night as the others set up camp.

"I saw a man so thirsty that he killed his animal to drink the blood" Balthazar commented. Caspar prayed silently as they rode. He had asked Balthazar several times if the stars said anything, but time and time again Balthazar told him that they did not.

Scouring the land as they rode, the group had remained in camp, unable to move forward.

What if we all die of thirst? Balthazar wondered.

Melchior stayed back with the others. He reminded those in his sect that Moses had struck rocks and produced water. They continued to pray and hope. Many were becoming sick, too tired to move out.

Caspar wondered too. Silently he did the unthinkable. He prayed a silent prayer to Melchior's God. *Please help us.*

The next day, they found water. It was the great river, the Euphrates! They could follow this into Roman territory. This was the route traveled by traders; they would travel along the water until they reached the Roman cities.

When they came to a rise, Caspar said a silent prayer of thanks as he pointed. "There!"

Balthazar sighed with relief. They had found water!

There before them was a stream of glorious water. Both men cheered from happiness as they rode back to camp. They took a group of soldiers to fill large barrels to take water to the people. First they quenched their thirst, then they went in shifts to fill their empty containers and let their animals drink.

When they had drunk their fill, the people rested, and ate.

They camped for a few days by the side of the spring as they all regained strength. They set out again, moving along the river.

***

Balthazar rode with Caspar. Before the, journey, he had known Caspar, but the young Zoroastrian's leadership during the last few days had caused him to find a new respect for the magus.

"On this journey we have seen the best and the worst of ourselves. It is because we've had to face ourselves without distractions. Maybe that is why it has been so long." Caspar observed.

"My young friend is a philosopher!" Balthazar laughed. He had grown to have an affection for the younger man.

The journey had changed them. Even though they all were magi, they would not have spent time together back at home---an old magus, a young Zoroastrian, and a sky-watcher.

"We are Magi and it is our nature to believe in the sacred. We yearn for something bigger than ourselves and it is not enough to stop at the first thing. I know you believe in what you have been taught, so do I. No, I have searched and questioned and it has led me here to where I am. I do not have to see this child to know that he is the one that I have waited for my whole life. I know. When you keep searching and searching, you come to the truth. Maybe Bardan will find his answers if he keeps searching."

"Perhaps. Sometimes, I admire Melchior's faith. He does not go to see *if* this child is who the stars say he is. No, he goes because he *knows* it to be true."

"In some ways we are totally and profoundly different, especially in the way we see ourselves in relation to the divine. As magi, our sects hold different beliefs. This is true, but there is something that unites us as well. We look for things beyond what we see and we believe in something greater…Even you, Balthazar."

"I don't know if I believe in anything at all."

Even if you look only in yourself, there is a spark of a divine there. Look at the fire. You know it well, what happens when even the smallest of sparks ignites?

"The fire grows."

"Exactly."

"I have no doubt that God has plans for you my friend..."

But which one, Caspar wondered

I wonder, Balthazar thought to himself.

LOSING THE STAR

Balthazar called the other two men into the tent. His face was pale and his eyes were wide.

"I have lost the star."

"What do you mean?" Caspar asked him nervously.

"It just *disappeared.* I have looked for three days and I have not seen anything. I am not sure what to do."

Caspar could see how the responsibility of these people weighed on Balthazar.

"What should we do?" Balthazar asked the both of them. He looked at both men, younger and older.

"Do you think we should wait? Maybe the star will come back in a day or two." Caspar wondered aloud.

"*God* will deliver us." Melchior said. "He will not abandon us."

"There is no talking to YOU!" Balthazar exploded.

Every time there was a problem, Melchior would repeat that his God would not abandon them.

Melchior looked at him, shocked. He had never seen the

sky-watcher show so much emotion. This Balthazar reminded him so much of his son, Tigranes. Their eyes had that
same defiant resolve.

His tone softened, "I do not mean to offend you."

Balthazar sighed, "I know you do not, but we have a
problem, Melchior. People will die. Where is your God? We
have thousands of people who are looking to US to save
them. Should we call a council? At least we will have a few
more people helping us make a decision.

"Caspar, you want to light a fire and pray to your god,
while Melchior, you want to rely on prophecies and dreams.
Can either of you tell me to look into the sky. I have not seen
the star for two days. What are we going to do?"

"We should wait." Melchior said quietly. "The star was
from God. There is a reason it has disappeared."

"Melchior, the food is running out, who knows how long
we should wait."

"I was thinking," Caspar spoke, "That we should travel to
Rome since the king was not born in Parthia, perhaps he was
born in Rome. It is a powerful nation, a mighty empire fit for
a king."

"Perhaps" Melchior said slowly. Thinking over his words.

Caspar continued, "It is a place of learned men, industry
and soldiers. It is said that the Circus Maximus itself can
hold as many as two hundred and fifty thousand people for an
afternoon at the chariot races. Wouldn't a king be born in a
highly populated area?"

"But Caspar, power and wealth are not everything. What
about knowledge?" Balthazar countered, "I suppose Rome
does seem like the logical choice, but what about Athens? It
is the center for so much thought. We would have to get more
supplies if were to travel that far. What about the cities that
we do not know that might be further?"

"I have wondered if the star is leading us to Jerusalem,
the Jewish capitol," Melchior wondered aloud, "but still I do
not know."

"This is not helping" Balthazar fumed.

"He is correct; our theorizing is not getting us anywhere. I would prefer to wait, but since you do not, why don't we go to Jerusalem and ask? It is the closest city and King Herod will most likely know the location of the new king."

"And our people can rest and get supplies."

"Yes, for a short time, but we do not want to rest too long, we are so close, but I hope it will be our destination."

Balthazar was not expecting such a practical response from the old man. He nodded to him in appreciation. Caspar nodded as well. It seemed like a good plan.

JERUSALEM

They stopped when they saw Jerusalem in the distance. What he saw ahead brought hope to Melchior's heart. He thanked God for listening to his prayers and allowing them to gaze upon the holy city: Jerusalem. They had decided to leave the group camped a short distance outside the city. Balthazar, Bardan, Caspar and Melchior went ahead to seek information.

"We should approach the city carefully," Balthazar warned.

"Why should we hide?" Caspar asked. "We are not at war with Rome."

"Do not forget that in my lifetime Herod fought against our people." Melchior reminded them. "I am sure he is a just leader but we should go to the temple and ask. The worshippers they will know."

Caspar, Balthazar, Bardan, and Melchior entered Jerusalem. The city amazed Melchior. This was the city of David and of Solomon and he had even heard that Abraham had been there. The ground he walked upon was hallowed. Jerusalem was surrounded by a great wall to protect it from outsiders. They walked through the gates slowly, trying to blend in with the others. It was not easy, their garments and walk were out of place. As soon as they entered the gates they were seen by soldiers.

Two Roman soldiers walked up to the four men and asked, "Who are you?"

Caspar spoke quickly, "We are magi, members of the Parthian magistrate."

"Parthian!" the solider got up. "You are with the soldiers positioned outside the city?"

"We are, but the soldiers are only there for our protection."

"Wait here," the solider said gruffly. He went to speak with a group of soldiers. He walked toward a group of soldiers patrolling the outer wall of the city.

"There are four men here. They are obviously not soldiers. Should we alert the palace guard? Could they be spies?"

The other guard looked across the courtyard at the four,

"Their dress is undoubtedly Parthian. Look at the fabric of their garments, it is expensive. The palace should be alerted. They are either dignitaries or spies."

"I will detain them here until you return," the first solider replied.

They were kept with the soldiers while the messenger went to Herod's palace. The messenger came back with word to bring them to the palace. Four soldiers walked the men through the city streets. The members of the city were obviously agitated.

"Why are they so concerned?" Bardan whispered to Balthazar.

"I think they know that we are outside the city. Look, even the people are alarmed."

"They think they are being invaded!" Bardan concluded,

realizing that the whole city was in an uproar over their arrival.

"Obviously we are not invaders." Melchior dismissed the idea. However, Parthia and Rome were anything but allies. More than a generation ago, they had fought a bloody battle and there had been no true victor. Since then, the relations between the two kingdoms had been tense.

"How is it obvious to them? They don't know. They've lived through wars before. No wonder they are nervous. We should have sent riders ahead." Balthazar lamented.

They walked silently. Each wondering how this would end. Herod's palace was a sight to behold. It was not as great as Phraates', but it was huge for a diplomat. That was what he was, a diplomat appointed King of the Jews by Rome.

"This is a Jewish city?" Melchior asked aloud. It did not look Jewish to them.

"No, this city has the look of Rome."

They walked through large buildings separated by streets and palaces. It was impressive, they could not deny. It looked new, elaborately decorated. The buildings loomed over them, rising further and further into the sky.

THE SHEPHERDS

Esther wandered on the outskirts of the town. She too was feeling impatient. The past few weeks had been difficult and lonely. Left alone with her thoughts, her heart seemed to ache for Barden all the more. She worried for her grandfather, as well as the man she had hoped would embrace her God. While she walked, she prayed.

Dear Lord, please show us the way and show *Bardan the way to you.*

She had found it more and more difficult as the days passed to keep her mind off of Bardan. He had cared for her comfort and well-being. Her heart broke for him. He did not know the comfort she knew. Maybe he was a distraction. She had asked God to send her a helpmate and if it was to be Bardan then she would know. If not, then God would have a better plan. She would have to trust.

Even when it was difficult as it was in that moment. Walking away from the caravan, she looked out at the beauty that lay before her. That was the great city that she had heard so much about. Within those walls the new king might be sleeping.

She saw a few young boys looking at the caravan from a distance. They looked harmless, but curious.

"Hello."

"They shyly looked at her then spoke back. She was thankful they understood her. One boy hid behind the other two. The slightly taller one stepped forward.

"Why are you here?" Ardok asked her.

"To worship the new king" Ether said simply. Ardock's eyes widened.

"What do you mean?" he asked suspiciously.

"We have come from a land far away, Parthia. Our sky-watchers have been following the stars. We've been traveling for many months to visit the new king that has been born, perhaps in this city."

He smiled and looked at his friend as if he knew the story.

"My name is Shem," one of them said, "this is Aryahu and Ardok."

"It is a pleasure to meet you," she said.

"The new king is not in this city," Aryahu volunteered.

Before she could ask a question, Ardock began to speak,

"It was more than a year ago. My brother Sunil was supposed to help my cousin Aryahu with the sheep but he was not feeling well. I did not want to go, but my brother persuaded me. I will never forget. We were out tending our sheep. It was dark. Then the light began to grow."

Shem added, "Then we could hear them."

Aryahu interjected excitedly, "We heard the earth and sky rumble. It was the angels' voices. Then we saw them. It was... so beautiful!"

Ardock pulled his cloak close around his ears. "I wish that I could have seen them again."

"They led us to where a baby slumbered." Shem continued.

Esther's heart pounded with excitement. She saw the

glow in their eyes and it was evident that something mystical had happened to them. Leaning in she listened with every fiber of her being.

"It was a small child, born in the lower part of a house amongst the animals. Laid in a manger,"

A manger? This could not be.

His eyes glowed as he spoke, "Everything changed that night. Everything. I still cannot sleep hoping the angels will return."

"Were you afraid of the angels?" she asked.

"They were large, larger than the largest man I know and strong. They had six wings and eyes that could see, everywhere. But most of all they were beautiful. First I was afraid, but then I felt at peace. There was no denying they were who they say they were."

"I said to my cousin, how could it be that an angel would come to us? We are just shepherds. We have never spoken to a king, and rarely seen one." Aryahu recalled.

"We had nothing to offer him," Shem explained.

"But when we saw him, we knew what he wanted." Ardock interjected.

Esther's heart began to beat quickly. What could this young king want? "What? What did he want?"

"I don't know how he asked, he did not speak, but somehow, somehow he asked me for everything," Ardock said carefully.

"I do not understand. Explain." Esther begged.

"I do not either. Every king I know assumes all that we have is his. Our parents have paid taxes to Caesar. This king asked for everything, but demanded nothing. He asked for more than just what we had."

What did this mean? What king would not want some sort of offering? Could it be that he had so much he did not need anything? Then why was he born in a manger?

She could not understand any of this. Her mind and her heart debated.

"He wanted our hearts and our minds," Shem explained.

"Yes, Yes," the others agreed quickly.

He was the *ONE!* The God of Abraham, Isaac, and Jacob had kept his promise. He was the Jewish God. The one she had heard so much about that yearned for the love of His people.

She could not wait to tell her grandfather....and Bardan. It was a strange message and she could not understand the entire message. How could a king ask for everything. The meeting had given her hope. It was no coincidence that the shepherd boys were near the city that night. It was not by chance that they had met her. No, they were a gift to her and so, there would be no more doubt.

KING HEROD

The city was unlike any other. From far away, they could see the retaining walls around the Temple Mount.

"Why is the temple so large?" Caspar wondered aloud.

"There are seven million Jews that live in the Roman Empire and some in Persia. They come here to worship during the Passover, Shavuot and Sukkot, the high holy days. That is why it is so large."

"It was the temple I saw in the distance!" Balthazar explained, "I thought it was a mountain covered with snow!"

As they entered the Eastern gate, soldiers immediately surrounded them.

The tallest one, obviously the leader, spoke to them in Latin, "Who are you?"

Balthazar became the spokesmen, though all the men understood his words, "We are here, visiting."

"What is the purpose of your visit?"

"We have come to worship the new king," Caspar said

immediately.

"New king? There is no new king? You came to see King Herod?"

"Herod?" No. Melchior had heard of Herod. He was an Idumean, named king by Augustus.

There were rumors among the Parthians that said Herod was ruthless and paranoid. They had heard that he, like Phraates, had killed members of his family.

"Look at how they are dressed," one said to the other.

"They came with the army camped outside the city," the other soldier observed.

"We are members of the Parthian magistrate," Bardan interjected; surely they would respect their position.

"*Parthian?*"

"We must get word to the king," one mentioned to the other.

"No," the leader said "Take them to the palace. I am sure that they will want to see these...magi."

And so they were led through the street. As they moved closer the temple became more visible. It was on top of a platform, perched high above the city. Dazzling, it was entirely covered in *gold*. The guards led them further to another equally impressive building.

This was Herod's palace, named the Herodium.

Constructed on top of a hill, it was a circular palace, that rose sixty meters above its surroundings. The base was built from large marble, so closely placed it looked as if it were one huge wall of stone. Huge towers projected from the walls on all four sides. The eastern tower, the largest, was a massive, round tower on a solid stone base.

The entry-gate to the fortress, in the northeast, was reached via a straight, steep staircase within a corridor built into the earthen rampart. Imposing it stood, not only as a palace but also as a fortress, designed to keep out all invaders.

The magi grew nervous as they were led through the palace gates and into the palace itself. They moved through the building and finally were led inside to a room adorned with Roman statues and great tapestries. Every surface seemed to be covered with gold or marble.

"This is a fine palace," Bardan remarked.

Melchior agreed. *I wonder---what will the palace of the new king will look like? Greater. Undoubtedly.*

The soldier brought them inside a room then spoke to the man dressed in long, robes. He was not King Herod, but they could not tell who he was. The man walked over and asked them,

"Why are you here?"

Melchior answered first, "To worship he who is born king of the Jews."

This was confusing to Ladus. Herod was the king of the Jews and he had been born many years ago. If anything he was closer to death. Even at that moment Herod had made Ladus his emissary, greeting everyone that passed through the doors so he did not have to trouble himself. Herod's health was failing and so he was becoming more and more paranoid of those that surrounded him. What could this man mean? Worship?

"I do not understand what you mean. There is no new king."

"We have been looking for a new king. We followed a star from our kingdom."

"Your kingdom?" He looked at the men. It was apparent that they were men of wealth and high rank.

"We are magi from Parthia," Caspar announced proudly.

Ladus realized what this meant. Parthia was not an obscure land. The powers and wisdom of these Parthian magi were known throughout the kingdoms. Some were wealthier than kings and they had the ear of the great Phraates. If word got back to Phraates that Herod had not treated them well then he would be in trouble.

"Please, come in and sit down."

Ladus welcomed them in and when they had been seated,

he sent for food and drink to be brought out immediately.

"I have not heard this story; please tell me so I can tell King Herod."

They told him of the star and their journey. When they had finished their story, Ladus immediately stood up. He had never heard a story like this one the men told. First, he would show them hospitality worthy of royal guests. It was his duty, honor and pleasure.

"You must be tired from your long journey. Come, rest awhile. I know the king would like to speak with you. I must tell him the glorious details of your travel. We shall have a feast made in your honor. It is not often that we get esteemed guests from Parthia visiting us. I know that King Herod would be greatly offended if you did not dine with him tonight."

He left and the magi sat in silence. Melchior did not know what to do. Had he led all these people astray?

A fine assortment of food was brought out for the men. King Herod was too ill to meet with company. Ladus usually entertained the guests with fine food and relayed their messages to the king, if necessary.

Disturbed by the news, he immediately ran to tell his master. Herod was ailing, but there was a fire that still burned in his eyes. Death would have to wrestle with him, he would fight back-what other choice did he have.

Ladus entered the king's bedroom quickly. King Herod lay on the bed, his pallor was white and he was sweating profusely.

"What is it Ladus?" He growled. Even now, Herod was interested in all the matters of his kingdom. Cruel and ambitious, he had made himself a king and a conqueror.

Ladus hesitated for a moment. He knew that this message would cause bloodshed. Whenever the king would hear a rumor that there was an attempt to take over his throne, he would kill that person first. Then go into depression. After awhile he would come out of his depression and would

build, build, build. Ladus had seen this cycle repeated itself
a number of times in which numerous people were killed,
including one of Herod's ten wives as well as three of his
sons. However, it was a valuable piece of information so he
King Herod.

"Worship the new king? *What new king?*"

"I do not know. They say that they followed a star---that
a new Jewish king had been foretold in some prophecy. Sir,
they are Parthian magi, they can appoint anyone the new
king."

Anyone? An anger immediately grew inside of him and
prompted him to get up. No one would take his throne away
from him! The anger coursed through his veins and enabled
him to get up. He was ailing but he would meet with these
men, see them first hand.

"I will prepare. I need to find out more about this new
king…Ladus, we must treat these men well. Relations with
Parthia have been tense and Augustus would not look well
upon us if we were the cause of any issue between our kingdoms.. Send patrols of soldiers out so they can survey the
size of their army. It will do us well to be prepared."

***

Ladus had the palace guard move the four magi to an oc-
tagonal room at the center of the western hall. This room was
magnificent, it had walls decorated with plasters and frescos.
It is assumed that this room served as a reception hall, or
perhaps even as the king's throne room when he received
dignitaries, the Jewish leaders and his subjects.

Compared to the rest of the palace it was of modest
dimensions. However, it was even more impressive than the
rest of the palace. It had floors of colored tiles, mosaics and
wall paintings and included every imaginable feature for
comfort.

Melchior had been growing more upset since they had

entered the city. He had been lamenting the circumstances. There were millions of Jews in the city. *If a new king was born, how did they not know? Why was Herod still in command? Could Daniel have been wrong?*

In that moment, ironically, it was Bardan who had the most faith. His vision has showed him that this king *had come* and *was powerful*, much more powerful than Phraates, Herod, or even Augustus Caesar.

Two attendants entered the room and stood at attention. Ladus followed then slowly, Herod walked into the room. His garments were as fine of those of King Phraates.

Herod had always enjoyed the finer things in life. When he visited Rome, he would collect art and clothes to bring back to Jerusalem.

"Do you like my palace?" he asked. His voice was smooth. Looking at each of them, he took stock of each.

"Did you know that you can see much from my palace overlooking the Judean Desert and the mountains of Moab to the east, and the Judean Hills to the west? I built it here to commemorate my victory over our Hasmodean and Parthian enemies. It was in this very spot where I won the victory. I call it the *Herodium*."

They nodded, not knowing what to say. Herod continued to speak, now seated on a comfortable throne. "Did you see the towers when you came in?"

"Yes, they are impressive." Balthazar had noticed them from a distance. They were much higher than those in his temple in Parthia.

"I have named them Hippicus, after my father, Phasael after a friend of mine, and the third Mariamne."

Caspar gave Balthazar a quick look. He remembered his father speaking of this king. Mariamne was his wife, whom he had killed. It was better not to mention that fact. As Parthians they had learned that though it was commonplace for the royals to murder each other, they took offense when anyone else mentioned the fact.

"You must come up to the eastern tower. As astrologers, you could properly appreciate its height. Undoubtedly you saw it when you arrived. It rises above the entire fortress. From my tower I have an excellent panoramic view."

Balthazar wondered if he could find the star from that height.

"Ladus told me that you were coming to see a new king?"

"Yes, we have traveled far to see him."

"I have not heard about this new king. There is no new king in the entire Roman Empire."

"But the stars and the prophecy have led us this far," Caspar offered.

Herod knew this was true and though prophecies could be wrong, he could not take the chance that this one was correct. These men had traveled far, and all of Jerusalem knew of their presence. It was a large city, but news of soldiers outside the city gates would spread quickly.

"Yes, the prophecy has been handed down for hundreds of years and spoke of a new *Jewish* king."

A new Jewish king? Herod heard the words but pretended that he had not.

"You must be tired from your long trip. I can have a feast prepared."

"Thank you for your kindness, King Herod." Melchior was impressed by the generosity of the King. He had welcomed them. The temple had been rebuilt under his command and it was beautiful, "but we need to continue our search."

"Come, come, what is your hurry? I have every sort of convenience you can imagine. I have gardens, beautiful gardens, artwork that is to be admired, if you would like to rest after your long journey. I have room to accommodate at least a hundred of your men. It has a bathhouse and a pool."

They were tempted, very tempted. Melchior wanted to stay, but he thought of Esther and the others. They were outside the city waiting for them and it was his responsibility to lead them.

"We cannot stay, there are others waiting for us."

The king nodded. He knew that they would not stay but it did not matter. "Let me give you some supplies for your journey and I will have soldiers bring you water. I would come with you, but as you can tell, I am in poor health. Please, come back and tell me where this new king is so that I too can worship."

Melchior looked at King Herod. He was a noble leader.

"Yes, of course we will. It will be my honor to tell you where to worship."

"Then I appoint you plenipotentiaries of the Kingdom of Judea. As we prepare the food and water; you must look at my garden. Ladus, you lead the men. Balthazar, I will have a guard lead you to the tower."

When Melchior, Caspar, and Balthazar had moved out of the room Herod spoke, "Bardan, could I speak with you?"

Surprised the king knew his name the young magus nodded.

"Tell me, what is your expertise?"

"I can predict the future." It was a bold statement and not entirely untrue.

"I would be honored if you would consider coming back and becoming one of my advisors. You would be handsomely rewarded, of course." He paused then asked, "Can you tell me something about this new king?"

Bardan's face immediately clouded. *What would he tell him---that the child would threaten all he knew?*

"I have had a vision of this king," Bardan offered hesitantly.

Herod looked mildly impressed. "Continue," he commanded.

"I can tell you that he is very powerful. He will make… changes."

Herod began to look uncomfortable. Bardan decided not to tell him more. It was obvious that Herod was hungry for power. Bardan could use his insight to have a higher position in Jerusalem than he could ever aspire to back home.

Now, he had nothing to tie him to Parthia. Esther's face came to his mind, but he pushed it away quickly.

"I could use a potion to tell you more, but it will take more time."

"No, no I would never take you away from your quest. I need you to go and come back. Let me know where to go, so I too can worship and bring him gifts."

Bardan watched the king's face. The look in the king's eye gave him a chill. It was almost sinister. In that moment, he realized what King Herod was asking. He planned to kill the child.

This would be his first task. If Bardan returned with the information, he would have a life of power and riches.

As soon as the magi left, Herod called for his Jewish advisors.

FINDING THE STAR

A s they made their way back toward the encampment, Esther ran toward them with excitement. She told them about the shepherds and what they said.

Bardan seemed unusually interested in her words.

"Where did they say this king was born?

"Bethlehem."

"I have never heard of this place. Beth Lehem?" Melchior muttered. He was now despondent. Beth Lehem meant "house of bread". How could the promised one who was sent to be the greatest leader, to free them from their oppressors be born in such an obscure and insignificant place?

Esther looked at her grandfather. Why was he acting strangely? She expected him to be as excited as she was.

"Do we know where this Bethlehem is?" Caspar asked.

"No, but we should ask King Herod. He would show us the direction." Balthazar offered.

Bardan did not like this idea. He wanted to prove his worth to Herod. "No, that is not a wise idea," he offered. "We are ambassadors from Parthia. If we trust the word of these shepherd boys and tell King Herod what will happen to us if the child is not found. They will think us to be fools."

The men nodded in agreement. They would have to find another way.

"Esther, can you find these boys? They can lead us." Caspar suggested.

"I will go with her," Bardan volunteered.

She looked up, startled. Bardan wanted to go with her? Immediately they left the tent and began to look around. It was dusk and nightfall would soon be there.

"We may have to look tomorrow," Esther offered. Her heart was beating loudly in her chest and as she walked she continued to pray.

Bardan nodded, "We may, but let us use the light for as long as we can."

They searched, saying nothing. "I remember they left in that direction." She told him as she pointed. "We should start there."

He nodded his head and followed her.

As they walked Esther took a deep breath, "You have treated me unfairly, Bardan."

Bardan looked at her, surprised at her words.

She continued, "You were my friend and you took that friendship away. You told me you did not want to marry me. I can understand your reasoning. I, too, do not want to marry a man who does not love God---the one true God. That doesn't mean that I did not mourn our friendship. It may be fruitless and improper for a man and woman to be friends, but I did enjoy our conversations."

She looked at him, trying to hold back tears, then asked, "Bardan, is there any part of your heart that can believe in my God?"

Bardan looked at her.

Her God? How could he believe in her God?

"Why then, why did you make this journey Bardan? I know that I asked you to go, but if you thought so little of me, why did you decide to come? Do you believe that we will find the king?

This he could answer. This he had to answer. He wanted to find this king just as much, if not more, than she did.

"I do believe that a king has been born," he answered.

She looked at him, dumbfounded. If he believed this maybe that was all he needed. She had seen the shepherd boys. If Bardan saw the new king, he would believe in God. The shepherd boys had been transformed. They sang the praises of God. Her heart began to dance with hope.

Esther stood watching the setting of the evening sun. She prayed, begging God to show them His mercy. They were so close, and had traveled so far. Bardan watched her. She was, indeed, the most beautiful woman he had ever seen. He closed his heart, filling it with contempt for her and her God. They had caused him this pain and they were the ones that sought to destroy him and all he knew.

***

Sitting in the darkness, Melchior buried his face in his arms. What had happened to them? It could not be his king. Esther had said that they laid him in a manger? *A manger?* God would not allow his new king to be treated worse than a peasant. No, it could not be. The prophecy had been God's promise. His ancestors had put their lives in service of this promise. He had believed in the prophecy.

Since he was a boy, he had yearned for this day. He had imagined himself as one of Daniel's companions and sometimes even a servant of the great Moses. What would it have been like to have such a close encounter with God? He would witness the fulfillment of the prophecy---a king who would be enough for him.

Should he still trust? Maybe he had lived his whole life as a fool. The Romans had brought suppression to the people of Israel. Even he had known that. He had imagined a great king who would raise an army and wipe out all those that would suppress his people. Melchior would not live to see the day, no, but if he could see the face of the man who would bring his people peace. He wanted to see the deliverer.

Even in Parthia, he had heard his people crying out for rescue from Roman oppression. That is why Tigranes had left to fight.

He still had to believe that someday, God would send *the* deliverer, the *promised* Messiah. *Oh, Lord, was this all in vain? I want to believe, but I have traveled so far and doubt has entered my heart. Please take away the doubt!*

Esther and Bardan did not find the shepherds that night. They decided to resume their search in the morning. As soon as they returned, Bardan went to visit Avashya. Under the cover of darkness, he made his way quickly to her tent. She was still awake.

"I have been expecting you Bardan," she said.

"Do you know why I have come?"

"I know you have made a powerful ally."

"They say the child is in a place called Beth Lehem? Can you find this place?"

"You can see it as easily as I can, have you looked into the mist and asked the spirits?"

"No, I have not had time."

"Ah, you should have me look…" He nodded, it was easier to have her look.

She got up and gathered a few glass bottles. Pouring drops from each into a bowl, she closed her eyes and started to chant in a language Bardan did not recognize. He waited.

Avashya opened her eyes, as she looked up, she began to weep. She moaned a low, painful moan as if what she had seen had physically wounded her.

"You have seen our doom?"

"I have seen the land covered with the blood of the in-nocents. Children slaughtered…mothers wailing in agony." Her face contorted as she recalled the scenes.

"What? Where?"

"In Bethlehem," she whispered.

He did not know what it could mean.

"Will this new king cause this slaughter? Is this the symbol of our ruin?"

"I do not know. I do not know how to interpret this vision. I do know that this king will change everything, but I do not know what this vision means."

He nodded, "If you find the location of the place Bethlehem, go to King Herod and tell him. Tell him that I sent you."

***

Melchior sat up for many hours praying. *Why have you brought us here God? Are you there or is this a fool's errand?* He could not imagine that God had brought them there to abandon them. He had to continue, even though it was difficult, but he did not understand. For hours he wrestled with his thoughts until he finally fell asleep.

Balthazar was slightly relieved that they were no longer traveling away from food and water. Now they were safe. He never expected to find anything and soon they would have to travel home. He thought about how it would feel to sit in his window and watch his familiar stars as he drifted off to sleep.

Caspar stood in front of the fire, searching for peace and answers. It would come. It had to come. He could not go home this way. No, now that he had learned so much. He was not ready to come home with nothing to show. He believed that there was something out there.

But where?

THE DREAM

Melchior, Balthazar and Caspar all dreamed that night. In fact, they had the same dream, though none of them saw the others in their sleep.

They each saw the figure of man standing before them. He was unlike any man they had ever encountered. Over seven feet tall and imposing, he stood silently. They could feel the strength of his presence from across the room. Dressed as a solider of the highest rank he stood at attention as six giant wings erupted from his enormous back. He looked directly at them and they knew that it was an angel of God that stood before them.

They were outside time and place, they gazed into the angel's eyes themselves. Somehow, he lifted them up with his eyes. Within his gaze they also saw a mighty fire. They each had known warriors and crazed men that had the fire of battle in their eyes. The fire had consumed those men, but this fire came from another place. It was inextinguishable and focused.

He addressed them, speaking their name. It was as if this was the first time their name had ever been spoken. Their name resounded within them long after it was spoken, stirring up feelings that had long died. They had been branded with their own name, and there was a purpose that came with the branding.

"Do not be frightened! I am a messenger sent from He who has created all things visible and invisible. I bring you good news. You will find whom you seek!"

The angel continued to speak. "Do not return to Herod's palace. Return home by another route. This man wishes to do the child harm."

Though they wanted to stay with him and sleep for a thousand years, they awoke the next morning, refreshed.

Melchior immediately threw himself prostrate on the ground and thanked God for his faithfulness. The dream filled his heart with hope. God had kept his promise.

***

As soon as the dream was over they immediately awoke. Balthazar's tent was filled with so much light he thought it was morning. Peering out of his tent, he was surprised to see that it was still night. The light was coming from the sky.

It was a star! It hovered low in the sky as if it was waiting for them. He reached out, attempting to touch it, but it was much too far. It was beautiful and he stood, awestruck watching for a few moments. When he regained his senses he went to tell Melchior, Caspar and Bardan. They, along with Esther, rode ahead of the caravan.

Melchior instructed the others to follow, knowing it would take time to get the great caravan moving. He spoke to the others as they walked.

"Last night I had a dream that has given me much hope."

Caspar responded, "I, too, had a dream. There was a great and powerful celestial being that spoke to me."

"There was a great messenger in my dream as well! He warned me not to go back to Herod.

"The being in my dream gave me the same message!"

How could this be? Balthazar was at a loss. How did they know his dream?

Melchior and Caspar spoke excitedly to each other as they walked. No one thought to speak to Balthazar who quietly listened to the details. His dream was exactly as the other two had described.

Bardan, too, listened to the description of the dream. What could this mean? How could he get word to Herod?

The men carried small gifts with them as they walked. They were only small tokens of the greater gifts that would follow with the caravan. These were the great gifts that Melchior claimed were for a "Messiah, Prophet, Priest and King" and that Daniel himself had left gold, frankincense and myrrh.

Balthazar reflected on the significance of the gifts. These gifts were rich in symbolism. The gold signified royalty as he was a king, the frankincense spoke of his priesthood, and the myrrh...he did not know the symbolism of myrrh.

Balthazar whispered to Bardan, "Do you know the symbolism of myrrh? I thought they used it as an embalming spice. Why would they bring this as a gift?"

Bardan shook his head, claiming ignorance, but he knew what he had seen. This baby would die. If he was not stopped, it would mean the ruin of everything he knew.

* * *

As she walked, Esther continued to pray for Bardan. She knew that God was working on his heart. How could he deny that God was glorious? They were following the most magnificent thing she had ever seen.

They were going to see their new king. Melchior had memorized Daniel's words. He knew of the power of dreams but never before had he experienced a dream from God. His God has spoken to him and had pushed him forward. There was no need for him to find the child to have faith; he knew the child was there. He begged God for forgiveness for all his doubt. Soon he would see the king!

Caspar wondered what this meant. Obviously there was more to this than he could imagine. His father had been worried that Melchior would convert people to his God. He had been sent to dissuade them. What if Melchior's God was converting *him?* He could not deny the power of the dream that had happened the night before. Dreams were sacred, he knew that and now, now they were following the most brilliant star he had ever seen.

THE EPIPHANY

They had followed the star through the night, walking over forty-eight furlongs. *This is no ordinary star,* Balthazar reflected. It fascinated him. The contained light was beyond anything he could understand or explain. Yet, it stood before him, piercing his heart. The unexplained beauty of the experience unified the small group.

Finally, in early light of dawn, they came to the house. The star hovered above the house. There was no need for words. They knew they had reached their destination.

The magi, who had moved across the face of the earth as though a mighty wind pushed them, now stopped. They were certain they had come to the right place. It was as though the voice of the Eternal God had spoken aloud: *He is here!*

Balthazar fixed his gaze on the star that hovered above this house. It was not a star, no, but it was so brilliant that he could not tear his eyes away. It spoke to his heart. *The child, the Son of the Living God . . . the baby you have come to worship . . . the stars are His! He made them all! He knows them each by name!*

Melchior knew the end of his quest breathed within this humble home. Though he had been so distraught the night before, now he was at ease. The house certainly was not that of a king, or even a noble. Still, he *knew* a king dwelt inside.

There is a moment before great change when everything is silent. That is the last moment of things as they are. Then, the world changes radically, shattering the reality that was. He stood now on the precipice of that moment.

Esther waited for her grandfather to knock on the door. In a few moments she would see him, the one she had dreamt about years before he was born. Her heart raced at the thought.

Melchior knocked on the wooden door.

***

When Joseph opened the door, Mary heard a voice speaking in heavily accented Aramaic. She heard Joseph say yes, and the men cry out happily. Joseph glanced back at her, his eyes bright but unsure.

"These men have come from the East."

"Who are they?" she asked, slightly afraid for her child.

"There are five of them. Four magi and a woman. They've been following a new star they say announces the birth of the King of the Jews. They've come to worship him."

She nodded, "Then we must let them worship."

Mary had grown accustomed to unusual visitors: the angel, the shepherds, and even the seers in the temple.

"They're Gentiles, Mary, and will defile the house."

"They know who he is. God himself must have sent them."

"Yes, I believe he has." Joseph nodded. Turning back, he opened the door wider. The group entered the small house. Mary and Joseph welcomed them.

"His name is Yeshua," the young mother said lovingly as she showed them her son.

The toddler smiled at the new visitors. The light in his eyes reminded the men of the angel in their dream. Mary drew back to give them more room. They stared at Yeshua with a mingling of joy and awe. One by one, they knelt and bowed their heads to the ground before him. Bardan and Esther stood back against the wall, allowing the other three to pay him homage.

"We have brought gifts," Caspar spoke, knowing the custom to give gifts to a king. He drew from his robes and elaborately carved box. Opening it, he showed Mary that it was filled with gold coins. She only had seen that much money at the table of the money changers in the Temple. Joseph too had never seen so much money in the hands of one person. It was more than he would make in his lifetime.

Melchior handed her an embroidered leather bag. "Frankincense," he explained as she took the bag. She looked at the old man sweetly as she handed the bag to Joseph. It, also, was more precious than anything that she could imagine.

Melchior had given both Caspar and Balthazar gifts to present, having three to give. Balthazar took the sealed alabaster bottle who awkwardly said, "myrrh" as he handed it to the beautiful young mother.

"We have much more of each gift," Melchior said. "They are coming with the others. These gifts have been kept for our king since the time of the great prophet Daniel, our Rab Mag."

Mary marveled at the gifts. Joseph handed each gift to Yeshua who took each, and then put them aside. They were new toys for his chubby hands to delight in as he touched them. He toddled among the men who had come to worship him, who still knelt on the ground. Smiling, he began touching their faces, and peering into their eyes.

Melchior wept openly when the child touched his face. Kissing his small hand he felt like a small boy before a man.

This child was no ordinary king.

Caspar also knew that there was something truly remarkable about the child. He had a feeling of peace unlike anything that he had ever experienced. Deeply moved after the dream, Caspar prayed as he had never prayed to the God who sent the angel, Melchior's God, who he had now chosen to serve. If this child was his chosen king, then he would follow.

Then Yeshua waddled over to Balthazar and looked into his eyes. Gazing, into the child's eyes, the magus realized that somehow this child had prompted him to speak in the temple months ago. This child was not just a king. He was *GOD*. He had heard Melchior use words like Adonai Elohim—Yahweh—the One God, the Almighty. Now he understood what those words meant. They were about *this child*. This flesh and bone child embodied all those names. It was beyond his understanding, but for the first time, he did not care.

As the other magi worshipped, Bardan watched the man they called Joseph. His hands were rough from work and his clothes were simple, not what he would have expected for the father of a king. *Why, he is my age!*

He felt a tug on his arm and looked down. It was Yeshua. This was the child Herod intended to kill.

Indeed, he had seen this child as a man in his vision. Yeshua looked into Bardan's eyes and for a moment Bardan had a vision more powerful than any he had ever known.

He gasped! Bardan's heart raced. Every moment was weaved into this one, every person he had ever known was held in the child's face.

Then he saw himself as he was. He could see the hurt and anger as a black ugliness that oozed out of his spirit. Try as he might, he could not hide from the child.

Then he saw himself through the child's eyes. Instantly, the anger and fear disappeared. Consumed by love, for an instant, Bardan stood without shame.

The vision ended and he fell to his knees. The child

placed his hand on Bardan's bowed head. Then, Bardan knew that his whole life is justified, his sins forgiven, and that his heart was able to love in a way that he had never imagined. All that he had clung to he laid before the child's feet. In an instant, he was transformed.

He heard an unseen choir singing. No one else in the room heard the words that were sung by thousands and thousands of voices:

"He is the image of the invisible God, the firstborn over all creation. For by him all things were created: things in heaven and on earth, visible and invisible, whether thrones or powers or rulers or authorities; all things were created by Him and for Him. He is before all things, and in Him all things hold together. And He is the head of the body, the Church; he is the Beginning and the Firstborn from among the dead, so that in everything he might have the supremacy. For God was pleased to have all His fullness dwell in Him, and through Him to reconcile to Himself all things, whether things on earth or things in heaven, by making peace through His blood, shed on the cross."

He had seen what the future held for the innocent that stood before him. He began to weep, first tears of sadness, then of joy.

Then Joseph spoke gently, "Come, be at ease. We don't have much, but what we have we offer you, but you are welcome to what we have." He poured wine and broke bread and listened with great interest as the men told them about their long journey to Judah. Bardan remained silent, watching everything in awe. Mary sat on the mat with Yeshua while he played with his wooden boat and animals. When Yeshua yawned, she took him up in her arms and gently laid him in a simple cradle his father, a carpenter, had fashioned from wood.

After the child was sleeping, Caspar spoke, "We went to

Herod and asked, 'Where is the newborn king of the Jews?' We told him about the new star, and how we had traveled so far to worship this newborn king."

Joseph's face was suddenly pale. "And what did King Herod say?"

"King Herod told us to go and search carefully for the child, and when we found him to go back and tell him so that he too could come and worship him."

Mary saw the fear come into Joseph's eyes. Bardan wanted to warn them but Melchior spoke before he could.

"Don't be troubled, Joseph," Melchior said. "A messenger of God came to us and warned us against returning to the palace."

Mary looked at Joseph, but his attention was fixed upon the men.

"Last night we all had the same dream." Melchior began.

"The exact same dream." Balthazar interjected as Caspar nodded.

Melchior continued, "We were all told not to return to Herod, but to go home by another route."

"Herod will seek you out," Joseph said grimly.

"He will send men to look for a company of magi with their servants, but he will not find us. Each of us will travel in a different direction: Babylon, Assyria, Macedonia, Persia and others. This will confuse Herod and you will have more time."

Bardan hoped that Avashya had not seen the location of Bethlehem. He prayed, You are more powerful, I know this now. Please cloud her vision so she cannot see.

***

You will have only a few days before the king realizes we have gone. Then he will begin hunting for the child."

The group sat with the small family and continued to talk. Esther watched the young couple and her heart ached. So many times she had seen young couples and wished that she too could know what it felt like to be in love. Love had made her feel alive. It has also made her feel a sadness she had never known possible. There had been times, she knew, when she wanted Bardan more than God's will.

The girl was younger than she was, though not by many years. Her heart was for her child, it was obvious, but also for the will of God. How she would have liked to have known this woman. She saw how she loved the child more than anything, it was clear that she put God first. Esther prayed, *"God I give you everything, you alone do I serve. No one, not Bardan or anyone else can take your place."*

She looked up and caught Bardan gazing at her. His face had changed, it was brighter. There was a look in his eyes that made her heart leap. In that moment she knew that he had fallen in love with God. Still, she prayed. *I have given you my heart God.* It is yours, direct me as you will.

In a quiet moment he came to her, "May I speak with you outside, Esther?"

She nodded. As she followed him, her heart began to pulse to the point she thought it burst from her breast. The bright cloud still stood above the house, making everything around her seem more brilliant.

"Esther," Bardan began, his eyes were glowing with a new fire. He took both of her hands into his and,. "I am sorry. I was afraid. There is no excuse I could give that could make up for how I treated you. I did not understand. Now I do."
Her heart leapt.

Tears began to fall from her eyes as he spoke. She was overcome with joy at the beauty of the moment.

"He is real. He is here." Tears were now falling from his eyes. She had led him to God, to a truth that he had never imagined possible. The idea of love had eluded him his entire life. Now, in a moment, the child had taught him what it was.

"It is because of you I have come so far. I would never have known…the Truth. " He had never wanted anyone else.

She had challenged him and inspired him more than any other. Long before this day he had wanted her to be his wife. Still, how could he convince her? What could he possibly say?

"Esther…I have a question to ask you…."

She was weeping when Bardan took her face in her hands. Esther could hear God speaking to her heart, loving her through this man that stood before her. Nodding, she accepted his proposal.

They looked up and saw the caravan moving toward them in the distance. Mary and Joseph came to the doorway and saw the immense caravan.

"Do all those people want to see our son? Mary asked.

"Yes," the oldest replied. "Perhaps you could take him outside and allow them to see the child." They nodded and rose. By this time Yeshua had woken from his nap. Before they left Melchior bestowed on the family the blessing of all those that had carried the prophecy of Daniel.

Generation upon generation spoke as one as Melchior declared, "May the God of your fathers watch over and protect you as you fulfill the prophecies that have been spoken by God into time."

He was pleased. There was a peace inside his heart that he had never known. He knew that his own child, Tigranes, was also loved and protected by this great God. They had seen him, real and wonderful. He did not understand how the Immortal One, who has existed since before time, can inhabit a mortal body. Still, he believed. It was the Messiah. He who would also be named Wonderful, Counselor, Mighty God, Everlasting Father and Prince of Peace.

Then the small family went outside to meet the crowd. As they stepped out, the magi proclaimed:

"He is our God!" Melchior sang out.

"He is our King!" Balthazar announced.

"He is our Lord!" Caspar proclaimed.

It was a mystical moment. The child walked slowly

through the crowd, taking a few steps then stumbling down. After a few feet his father scooped him up and walked him through the crowd. It was a sacred moment. "Forever and ever." *Our God reigns!*

Thousands joined them as they cried out in jubilation, hands reaching toward the heavens. They praised God for the new king that stood before them.

Caspar would call it a procession of the sacred or an encounter with the divine. For one moment, all were connected not just with each other but with all of time. The ache of loneliness that had plagued so many was alleviated as the child was in their midst.

As Caspar watched, he realized that this was not a re-incarnation no, this truly was the Messiah. He was entirely in the present, with no past, no future, absorbed in experiencing the morning, the music, the sweetness and the unexpected prayer. He entered a state of worship and ecstasy and gratitude for being in the world, glad that he had come on the journey. He felt a fire flooding his entire being. It was unlike any fire that he had ever felt. He had always understood that the divine revealed himself in the simple things---the stars, the wind, and especially the fire. Today, he saw God as a human child. He would call him "Emanuel" which meant "God is with us."

It was as Melchior has said. The man carried his son for a time, letting everyone see he whom they had traveled so long to see. They would fall into times of silence then the music would start up again.

They started to sing. At first it started with a few voices then slowly. . .slowly it began to grow. The deep tambour of the singing caused a vibration that could be felt throughout the crowd. These were the songs of their ancestors. Parthia was full of those with histories from other lands---Medes, Israel, Egypt and even further beyond. It was the songs of their ancestors, together, all praising the king not just of the Jews but of them all. Instantly, hearts were transformed.

The journey was by no means over, but they had found their destination.

EPILOGUE

They departed just as they said, following different routes to confuse Herod.

After the magi departed, an angel of the Lord appeared to Joseph in a dream. "Get up," he said, "take the child and his mother and escape to Egypt. Stay there until I tell you, for Herod is going to search for the child to kill him."

When Herod realized that the Magi, including Bardan, would not return to Jerusalem, he was furious. He gave orders to kill all the boys in Bethlehem and its vicinity who were two years old and under. And so, the Roman soldiers came and the children of Bethlehem were slaughtered. It was as Avashya had predicted. These children would be remembered through time as the Holy Innocents.

Bardan and Esther returned to Parthia. Some of the magi returned to their own ways, seeking power and practicing the old ways, but Bardan did not. He and Esther married, and happily raised a family. They lived in obscurity, continuing the tradition of Melchior. They passed down the story of their journey to their children with the intention that it be passed down from generation to generation.

These magi, now transformed, travelled through different towns and cities on their way home. As they moved, they shared stories about the baby Yeshua, also known as Jesus. They spoke of the Star, and all they had seen, heard and done. The magi traveled far and wide, proclaiming in places where they had never been. Because of this, many pagans left their errors and their false idols and worshiped this newborn child Jesus.

There is a story told that Balthazar built a beautiful chapel on the Hill of Vaus, in India, and sent word for Melchior and Caspar to meet there, and so they did.

Years later, the apostle Thomas came to preach in India. He told the people about Jesus's life, crucifixion, and resurrection.

Thomas preached this message in the temples of India, and performed many miracles by the sign of the cross. In every temple he entered he saw a star, which had been painted the likeness of the star that had appeared before the magi.

Seeing this, Thomas called for the magi and received them with great joy. The wise men told Thomas how they had gone to Bethlehem to see the baby Jesus and his holy parents. Even though Melchior was now a very old man, the encounter with the Christ child allowed him to remain alive, perhaps so that he could be baptized, with his two companions

The story is told that Thomas ordained these men as priests and bishops then went on to preach in other towns in India. In time he was martyred.

The magi, now bishops, taught about the life of Christ, ordained other priests and consecrated more bishops. Later, around the chapel of Vaus, the magi built the Catholic city of Suwella.

It is said that before their death a little while before Christmas, a wonderful star appeared above the city of Suwella. The star's appearance told them that they would die soon. So they built a large tomb in the church where they could be buried. They all said mass on Christmas day.

Eight days after Christmas, Melchior; who was 116 years old, said mass and then died. Three days later, Balthazar; who was 112 years old, said mass and then died. And six days later, Casper; who was 109 years old, said mass and also died.

The three wise men were buried there in their chapel. It is also said that years later, Saint Helen found these bodies and took them Constantinople, where her son was the Emperor. After the death of Saint Helen, the bodies of the three, were taken to Milan, Italy. Sometime later, Archbishop Rainald von Dassel took the bodies of the three magi to a church in Cologne, Germany, where they still are today.

BETHLEHEM

As you set out for Bethlehem,
Hope your road is a long one,
Full of adventure, full of discovery.
You will face giants---outside and inside,
As you face the giants, you will find your way.

Continue the journey,
Through the mountains and deserts,
When your companions leave you,
Continue the journey.

Your greatest threats lay with yourself,
Pride and Lust will nip at your heels,
And Shame will act as a millstone.
Face your Giants and they will have no power
Take them to Bethlehem and leave them there

Hope your road is a long one,
And that you see with new eyes,
The glory of the hardship,
The merit in the sacrifice.

May you see the colors of the sunrise and sunset,
Feel the deep silence of the sky.
Keep Bethlehem always as your destination.

On this journey you will learn,

The wise are wise only because they know Love.

The fools are foolish because they attempt to love without God

Bethlehem is a place, but it is also a marvelous journey.

It will take everything to get there,

But give you so much more.

ABOUT THE AUTHOR

Maryann Costa Beckman is a writer specializing in web copy, script writing, poetry and fiction. Her first novel, *The Secret of the Box*, is also an inspirational work of fiction that the whole family will enjoy. Maryann has written reviews and copy for numerous publications and websites. A graduate of Franciscan University with a Master's Degree in Business Administration, she lives in Southern California with her husband Joshua and is always at work on her next novel.

www.ingramcontent.com/pod-product-compliance
Lightning Source LLC
Chambersburg PA
CBHW020252150626
46552CB00020B/783